the secret people

B. R. Fleming

****

THE SECRET PEOPLE

After Thought Publications

The Secret People
Copyright © 2014 B.R. Fleming
First Edition: 2014

This is a work of fiction. Names, characters, businesses, places, events and incidents are either the products of the author's imagination or used in a fictitious manner. Any resemblance to actual persons, living or dead, or actual events is purely coincidental.

Fleming, B. R., 1949—
    The secret people/ by B. R. Fleming—1st ed.
        p. cm.
    ISBN-13: 978-0-9838201-1-6 (trade pbk.)
    ISBN-10: 0983820112 (trade pbk.)
    Library of Congress Control Number: 2014921492
    1. Adventure fiction—Fiction. 2. Native American
        spiritualism—Fiction. 3. Shamanism—Fiction. 4. Self-
        awakening—Fiction. I. Title.   813.087

Cover Design by Jeremy Fleming.
Book Design by Murdock Malone.
Photography by @BRImagery
        http://brimagery.wix.com/brimagery

Printed in USA.

Inspired by the works of Carlos Castaneda . . .

B. R. Fleming

CONTENTS

1

t'áátá'í

****

The hawk instinctively dipped, soared, dipped again in the updrafts created by the warming of the afternoon sun. Except for the invasion of the cliff walls below by the three intruders, the day would be like any other, soaring on the streams of air, searching for food, purveying the territory, unless the Airs made their presence known.

Of all the inhabitants of the canyon that day, only the hawk knew the ways of the Airs, the spirits of the wind who ruled the canyon and who tormented the spirits of earth and water. The intruders would know soon enough, too, of the tormenting ways of the Airs. The hawk had learned from the ancient ones, who had long ago discovered the ways to tame the treachery of the Airs, had mastered the art of gliding along with the currents, dipping and shifting course in a constant dance with the tricksters. Earth and water had no such luxury and bowed to the fury of the Airs, with no protection from the gusts that carried earth hither and thither and kept water from being at peace. Earth relaxed in the long-ago time and allowed the spirits of air and water to form the majestic canyon from its once solid presence, and now that formation had been preserved to be tested, tested by those who chose to intrude and challenge it.

The hawk's warning to advance cautiously echoed the canyon walls, falling on deaf ears. Its screeches only alerted the intruders of its existence riding the air currents above, to them a graceful, meaningless flight set against the dry afternoon, cloudless sky. Nothing to fear. No heed taken. No reason to abandon the climb. The hawk could only watch, and wait, and oversee, while the intruders continued their ascent. Instinct warned the hawk to keep its distance from the intruders, but a more heightened sense of impending menace drew the hawk to the small one, the weakest and most vulnerable of the three.

Lesley Whitney positioned herself on the rock, toyed with the lizard, intrigued by the lizard dance performed to repel attackers, to demonstrate his bravery. Instinct told the reptile that Lesley posed no threat but compelled him to engage in the enticing ritual, keeping her spellbound. Her presence there, alone with her father and her older brother, Conrad, occurred by accident anyway, and they just didn't understand her innate compulsion to explore everything around her, to delve into every crack and crevice. Her mom understood, had nurtured her curious nature, and would have encouraged her exploration had she not been taken ill at the last minute, remaining at home to rest.

Her father and brother continued their climb toward the ancient ruins carved into the canyon wall, their ultimate destination. Only the soft shale of the cliff wall delayed their persistent scaling of the slope, the same slope which contrastingly offered abundant crags and crevices that promised they would reach their goal. The ancient cliff dwelling lay far enough under the crest of the cliff, set back a sufficient distance into the cliff wall, to insure that very few, if any, others had made the trek up the wall to discover its secrets. That was the main motivation which had sparked Arthur Whitney to undertake the task, besides the fact that the grant money he had received necessitated that he pursue field studies. Bringing his son and daughter with him had been an afterthought, and his wife's suggestion, which he now wished had remained an afterthought, especially since his promise to take them had depended upon their mother coming along to watch over them.

Arthur wrestled the single lens reflex camera from his knapsack and documented his current position under the dwelling. The committee could always toss the documentation it felt non-essential, but Arthur knew from experience that one could never give them too much, only too little. Arthur had developed a formula for providing a carefully balanced amount and type of documentation which would assure that any committee's analysis of the materials could be accomplished in a "reasonable" time period, thus averting delays in receiving funding. However, the formula would be altered slightly on this trip with the presence of Conrad and Lesley and their desire to return with every rock, plant, or creature that they encountered.

Conrad had, of course, jumped at the opportunity to accompany his dad on the trip, hoping to be the "official documenter," but Arthur had been too pressed for time to adequately prepare him for those duties and had instead allowed him use of an old camera to be his "assistant documenter," a term Conrad proudly accepted, printing it on a presenter's badge Arthur had given him to pin on his shirt. The badge had since become Conrad's constant reminder to Lesley of his "official" status.

Conrad lost no time snapping shots of everything in sight, even though his dad had explained to him from the beginning that they only needed a "few shots" of the area leading up to the cliff dwelling. Every rock, twig, cloud formation, creature that appeared became his subject matter to fill his canvas, along with the shots his father asked him to take, which so far had been very few. He had even tried to get a shot of the hawk that had been flying overhead since they had entered the canyon, but the camera had mysteriously jammed when he pressed the shutter release. His favorite shots, though, thus far, had undoubtedly been of the coyote dung strewn along the path to the cliff, for which an entire roll of film had been snapped to thoroughly establish their presence in the canyon. The closer they came to the destination, the more he determined that he would need to limit himself, since only half of the rolls of film he had been allotted remained in the camera bag, and he would need all of that for when they reached the dwelling. When they finally got there, Lesley would most likely ask to use the camera too, even though he had assured her numerous times, pointing to the badge on his shirt, that he was the official "assistant documenter." His dad would, no doubt, tell him to "let her take a few shots." Eight-year-old sisters could be extremely annoying to fourteen-year-old boys.

"Conrad!" Arthur's voice from above startled Conrad.

"Yeah, Dad!" He looked up to see his dad perched on the boulder twenty yards ahead. "What's she doing down there?"

To Conrad, anything Lesley did interfered with the task at hand and with his time with his father. And seeing her sprawled on the rocks below made him wonder why his dad had ever brought her along. Well, he did know why she was there. His mom had insisted that she go along too "to be a part of the adventure" and had made Conrad promise to look after her, a job he reluctantly had agreed to perform when he couldn't convince his mom that his official job would be "too time-consuming to have to worry about Lesley!"

"I don't know. Can't we just go on up?"

"You know your mother wouldn't be too happy with us if we left her behind. Go down and get her."

As much as he wanted to just go on up with his dad, he knew that he couldn't leave her behind. If she got hurt, he really would never forgive himself, and his mom would use "the stare" every time she came around him to remind him of what he had, or hadn't, done. Dad was a little more understanding about those matters, but he wouldn't be too happy either if her getting hurt kept him from exploring the cliff dwelling.

"Les!" Maybe she was too far down to hear him. Or was it the wind blowing too loud for her to hear?

"Lesley!" He'd have to go down to get her, though he had used a lot of his energy to climb as far as he had.

Conrad cautiously began his decent, avoiding as much as possible the stretches of shale which had made the climb up so awkward and so time-consuming. The route he had devised skirted the looser shale and would be the one Lesley would need to follow to safely make the climb. Why couldn't she just kept up with them?

The lizard had made its way across the rock, avoiding Lesley's nudging, and had positioned itself on the edge of the outcrop, ready to make a quick escape, if necessary. Lesley followed the tiny creature with little thought that beyond the rock lay a straight drop down the shale siding of the canyon wall, wondering instead just exactly what the lizard intended to do once it reached the edge. Again, the lizard performed the fascinating dance, seemingly pleased with his capacity to seduce Lesley with the spectacle. With no warning, Conrad's slippery emergence from above broke the spell and caused the lizard to dart across the rock and into a crevice, leaving Lesley alone on the ledge.

"Lesley! We've been calling you. Come on! Dad's waiting for us!" Having delivered the message, Conrad wasted no time cruising back up the slope.

Lesley didn't want to end her adventure with the lizard but knew that her dad would not be too happy if they didn't make it to the ruins while it was still light. She hadn't tried to climb up the loose rock yet, keeping mainly to the many larger rocks which provided sure footing, but she would have to venture onto the loose rock if she wanted to catch up with Conrad and her dad.

"Coming." She tightened the straps on her backpack and stepped off the outcrop onto the shale and found that it wasn't as bad as she thought it would be. She just had to proceed a little more carefully to keep her footing. About ten yards ahead she noticed another outcrop and chose that as her goal to reach before Conrad had the chance to scream at her again to keep up. In true mountain goat form, he had already traveled way past that point, helping to establish a firmer footing for her, and would be watching to make sure she was following. Fourteen-year-old boys sure could be annoying to eight-year-old girls, but big brothers could somehow be reassuringly comforting.

Lesley drew a deep breath and followed step by careful step the path Conrad had revealed, becoming increasingly confident the further she scaled the cliff wall. Her goal began to appear too effortless with her new-found confidence, and another outcrop about ten yards further looked to be more reasonable to reach. She altered her course slightly, though it veered from Conrad's, and continued toward her new objective.

The break in the climb waiting for the kids to catch up had allowed Arthur a chance to make some notes. His thoughts had been dominated by reflection on the idea that this dwelling might be the one for which he had been searching for several years, though his investigation had so far been relegated to searching through documents and to journeying onto Hopi and Navajo reservations around the Four Corners and to Ute Mountain to listen to the stories told by the elders of the clans. Legend spoke of the time when Kokopelli, the hunchback flute-player spirit, had brought the knowledge of the art of dreaming to the Anasazi, the ancestors of the Hopi clans. This knowledge was sacred and would only be shared with the shaman of the clans, who would then share the knowledge with those they chose to retain the knowledge for future generations. The original Kiva, the ceremonial chamber of the Anasazi, where Kokopelli had emerged from the sipapu and taught the sacred art, was considered the most consecrated of all Kivas and had been kept secret to protect it. Other archaeologists had speculated that the Kiva could be found among the hundreds situated in the ruins of Canyon de Chelly or Chaco Culture or some other site in the Four Corners region, but Arthur believed that the Kiva was too important to be among the many found at those sites and that the Kiva had been part of a site from an even earlier time. For Arthur, finding this Kiva would assure him a rank of Full Professor of Archaeology and would add his name to the list of those who had made significant historical discoveries, like the Leakey's, Howard Carter, and Heinrich Schliemann.

The screeching of the hawk brought Arthur back in the moment. He returned the notebook to the knapsack, drank some of the water that had now warmed from the afternoon heat, and gathered himself to continue the climb. The kids appeared to be making good progress toward him and could just follow him the rest of the way to the dwelling. Conrad would make sure that his sister made it up the cliff okay, and he had assured his wife that he would keep Conrad on that task.

Conrad looked ahead and saw that his dad was again moving up the cliff , which made him even more anxious to catch up to be with him when he reached the site. After all, he had been assigned the job of helping to document the findings and would need to be there to do his job. The main thing on his mind at the moment, though, was how Lesley was slowing them down, and as he glanced back to see where she was, he noticed that she had strayed from the path he had set for her to follow. Why couldn't she just do like they asked?

Lesley had moved to a section which Conrad had particularly avoided, because of the deepness of the loose shale, and was almost running up the incline toward a huge boulder encased in the cliff wall. As she approached the boulder, a gust of wind blew through the canyon, and the loose shale gave way and sent her sliding back down the slope, grasping for something to break her slide. The loose rock carried her quickly down toward the outcrop where she had begun the ascent, and she landed awkwardly and rolled over the side, the strap of her backpack catching on a crag.

Conrad gazed in horror at the sight of his sister tumbling down the slope and dangling limply over the edge of the rock ledge, fearing that at any moment the strap would give way and send her plunging down the hundred foot drop to the canyon floor below.

"Dad! Dad!" Conrad hoped his dad wasn't too far above to hear him.

Hearing his son's cries struck fear in Arthur and caused him to turn to see the site feared most by any parent: seeing a child in danger. He cursed himself. Damn it all! How could this have happened? He could see Lesley hanging on the rock, limp, lifeless, and felt a shudder of utter helplessness pass through him. Conrad would need to get to her and keep her from falling any further while he made his way back down the cliff.

"Can you make it down to her?!"

"Yeah!"

"Hurry!"

Conrad raced down the slope using the loose rock to his advantage now to move even faster, knowing that the strap could give way at any moment. All thoughts of his sister's slow pace and refusal to follow instructions were now replaced with the single thought of keeping her safe. After all, he had made a promise, and promises had to be kept!

As he reached the outcrop, he saw that Lesley's strap had begun to loosen and had allowed her to move lower down the rock ledge. In order to reach her, he would have to hang over the edge and would need to hold on to something to keep from falling himself. He carefully straddled the edge of the ledge, finding a crag to hold onto, and reached with his free hand to grab the backpack strap and pull Lesley up to him. As he loosened Lesley from the snag, her weight and the weight of the pack together proved too much for him to lift her up to safety. He'd have to hold onto her until his dad made it down.

Arthur had gotten about half way down the hillside and could now see Conrad hanging over the side of the ledge, one arm on the outcrop and the other holding the strap of Lesley's backpack.

"Hold on, son! I'm almost there!"

"I've got the strap, dad!"

"Just hold it! Don't try to pull her up!"

Conrad had a grip on the strap, but now the weight of the pack and Lesley was beginning to take its toll on his arm. He knew he couldn't change hands in his current position, and his arm had begun to feel like limp spaghetti.

"Hurry, dad! I'm losing her!"

A pang of terror embraced Arthur. He still had nearly thirty yards to go before he reached the outcrop, and he didn't want to plunge down the hill and injure himself in his rush to reach the kids.

Then his worst fear came to pass. Shock overcame him as he stood helplessly and watched Conrad lose his grip on the rock and plunge downward into the loose shale below, rolling and tumbling until his body slammed into a boulder near the canyon floor. Conrad lay motionless. Was he dead? Where was Lesley?

Looking back to the outcrop he noticed Lesley again hanging from the rock ledge. Conrad had managed before his fall to reattach the strap to the rock, but how long she would last there was anyone's guess. He would have to pull her up to safety and then go to check on Conrad. How was he going to explain this to his wife?

The hawk had been keeping a watchful eye on the cliff wall and knew it could no longer keep its distance, eyeing the small one dangling precariously from the side of the outcrop, and quickly began its decent along the airways. As it approached the rock, a transformation began. Legs to arms. Feet to hands. The hawk's keen eyesight could now see the strap slipping from the crag and zoomed forward, gracefully enveloping the small one in its arms, gently placing her on the rock ledge above, and gliding effortlessly back into the midday sky, resuming its canyon watch, returning to its original form.

When Arthur reached the outcrop, to his amazement, Lesley lay on the ledge. He had fully expected to have to muster all of his reserve energy to pull her up to safety and wondered if the heat and the sun had made him see something different than what he thought he had seen. He glanced over the edge to see Conrad's still motionless body at the bottom of the slide. No. He hadn't imagined it. But how had Lesley managed to get herself up to the ledge?

He knelt and checked Lesley. She seemed okay. No obvious injuries. A few scratches and bruises, but otherwise looked alright. She moaned.

"Dad?"

He took some water from her canteen and patted her face, gently lifting her head to give her a drink.

"Lesley? Les? You'll be okay, Les. Don't move. I've got to get down to check on Conrad."

Lesley couldn't have moved even if she had wanted to right then. Her back felt like someone had stomped on it wearing hiking boots, and she was only slowly able to catch her breath. She opened her eyes and stared up at the open blue sky, her vision beginning to return, and wished she were back in her room at home having lunch with her cat. From now on she would leave the hiking and canyon climbing to her dad and Conrad. The pain in her back continued, and all she wanted now was to sleep. Conrad? Had she heard her dad say he was going down to check on Conrad? The screeches of the hawk interrupted her thoughts as it circled above, diving and floating on the canyon airways, and she drifted off into the darkness and safety of sleep.

B. R. Fleming

2

naaki

****

The screeching of the crane filled the air at the construction site next to the Hammer Health Sciences Building and could be heard for blocks, oftentimes terrifying students as they traversed the Columbia campus to their next class or to library research or to study group sessions or whatever. The professors in the offices and classrooms knew the construction was necessary for the new wing they needed, but they still wished that the construction could be done at night when fewer classes would be in session.

Lesley Whitney stood at the front of her students, in a classroom inside Hammer, in the middle of a lesson, mesmerized by the crane's rhythmic tune, and stared transfixed out the bay of windows into the clear blue summer sky. She'd heard that same melody before, and seemed to remember a similar blue sky associated with it, but from where and when had become lost in the torrent of childhood memories. She and her therapist had been slowly disengaging and reassembling the bits and pieces of events that she had "forgotten" for so many years, and moments like these helped to reconstruct the deep-seated memories.

"Dr. Whitney?" The students knew their professor could be distractible, but they had never seen her as preoccupied as she had been lately.

An air horn's blast announcing the noontime break sliced through the air and broke the trance. Lesley leapt back to reality and continued the lesson as if she had never stopped, using her remote device to control the holographic image in the middle of the lecture hall. The students glanced at each other around the room, grinning at their professor's ability to recover from her digressions.

". . . and we are making great progress in this area of assessment of inherited factors, including familial aggregation, phenotype definition, linkage analysis, and gene identification."

As she spoke, the terms appeared in the hologram with links to the cell images in the display. The students took notes on their Notepads, some snapping photos and videos of the hologram, as Lesley pressed another function button on the remote and changed the representation. Images of cells and labels for the cells and an organized array of arrows and other graphics now appeared in the hologram display area.

"Our current research has led to new revelations concerning gene LGI1 and its role in forms of temporal lobe epilepsy. We are specifically interested in the link between LGI1 mutations and inheritance of autosomal dominant partial epilepsy, or ADPE."

Lesley pushed another key on the remote, separating the hologram into two images, each with different cells and labels. She used the pointer on the remote to highlight the cell images.

"As you can see here, the T98G/vector showed high levels of phospho-ERK1/2 protein. In contrast, the T98G cells expressing LGI1 show a marked reduction in those protein levels.

These results lead us to believe that LGI1 mutations are a common cause of ADPE, most commonly with auditory features and sensory and psychic symptoms." Shutting down the hologram, Lesley moved to the front of the lecture hall to finish the session. She noticed a student with her hand raised in the back of the room. "Yes?"

"But Dr. Whitney, don't those same symptoms occur with seizures associated with brain tumors?"

"That's correct. And thus the conclusion that epilepsy can result from a myriad of causes, making our research as Epidemiologists even more complex and important. You can find the complete studies on my research web site or view the webinar. You'll need to complete the wiki on the class page before our next meeting here."

The tone to end class sounded, thrusting the students into a frenzy to shut down Notepads pack bags, gather belongings, and move on to their next class or work or mid-morning break or whatever task that next filled their schedules. Some gathered around Lesley to ask questions and make appointments, as usual, though she always reminded them that she had a Grad Assistant, Emily, who took care of those matters.

Lesley glanced at the clock and noticed it was also time for her to pack up and head to her appointment with the Dean; she waved the students away, reminding them to talk to Emily and wondered what Elliot wanted with her this time. Why couldn't they all just let her alone to do her research? Even teaching the lower level classes took valuable time away from her projects, but teaching responsibilities would always be a part of a university position. Research had always been her first love. Teaching classes and attending time-wasting meetings for meeting's sake were not her idea of being productive, a trait she, no doubt, had learned from her parents.

Her mother, Jacqueline, had been a full Professor in French Literature at NYU when she met Arthur Whitney, a Professor of Cultural Archaeology at Columbia. The phrase "opposites attract" always came to mind when Lesley remembered the two of them together. Though they indisputably loved each other desperately, their personalities collided, as did their views on politics and religion. Jacqueline had been raised Catholic in an upper class conservative family steeped in the political atmosphere of post-World War II France. Her father had served in the army under de Gaulle, and her mother had worked for the US Army as an Intelligence Analyst.

Arthur's family life couldn't have been more opposite. His father had served in the U. S. Navy as a Commander of a PT boat and his mother had worked in a psychiatric unit that treated soldiers suffering from "exhaustion", which later became known as Post Traumatic Stress Disorder. With an agnostic father and a mother raised in a half-Jewish household, religion took a back seat to politics and academia.

****

Strolling across the campus to the Rosenfield Building and her meeting with Elliot reminded Lesley of the times when Arthur would take her to the Columbia campus with him or to the dig sites he used to train his students. She would always be right there in the thick of it, grabbing tools for people, using the sifters, tagging the artifacts. Playing with other kids her age had never been high on her list of fun things to do. She loved being a part of the excitement of unearthing a clay pot or digging through a refuse pit. She had often heard Arthur tell his students that curiosity was one of the most important qualities a scientist could possess, and she had her share and more.

Entering the Mailman School of Public Health offices, Lesley felt the knot begin to tighten in her stomach as it always did at the antiseptic feel of the building. Elliot's office took up a sizeable chunk of the area allotted to the Dean's Offices in the building, but that included room for several office staff and Elliot's Administrative Assistant, Marta. Thankfully, Lesley didn't spend much time in the offices and had her own space in one of the older buildings in a remote section of the campus, where she relished the solitude, usually, and wasn't as likely to be inundated with students seeking answers to questions. Her grad students, especially Emily, could usually answer any questions the students had, and grad students had their own office spaces in the Hammer Building in the center of the campus.

"Hi, Dr. Whitney." Marta always referred to the professors by their titles, in case students were close by.

Lesley smiled and gave a little wave. "Is he in?"

"Be back in a jiff. Go on in."

Lesley settled into one of the chairs at a conference table and put her feet in the chair next to her. The Dean of the school being a friend of the family had its advantages. Elliot and Arthur had met while doing their grad work at the university and had written several papers together. Though they often disagreed on matters of policy, they had remained close friends and were known to share many a brew at the local pubs.

Outside, the constant, rhythmical hum of the construction equipment relaxed Lesley and lulled her into a daydream state. Her body eased into the contours of the chair, feeling lighter and lighter until total relaxation overcame her. She drifted off into a luxurious restfulness, a much needed relief from the tension she'd been experiencing lately. All of the seemingly thousands of memos, calendar events, notations, emails, phone messages, conversations raced through her head at light speed and slowly dissolved into a colorless, formless void. At the center of the void, an infinitesimal light began to emerge, spreading quickly in all directions, accompanied by a slowly, increasingly audible low frequency hum. Lesley struggled to free herself from the daydream but only became more entrenched the harder she struggled. The light now became flashes of piercingly brilliant streams flowing from all directions to all directions, traversing the black void, the low drone following in amplified bursts.

Panic seized Lesley. She was conscious enough to know what was happening but unable to move or to take control of the spectacle. The streams of light increased to the point that only minute specs of black remained interspersed on the screen in her mind. The low-frequency bursts had erupted into a constant roar like a freight train circling in her head. She had never felt such a complete loss of control before, yet, she could feel the presence of some force, some energy source manipulating the episode, thrusting her into the throes of a paradoxically sensual, almost ecstatic, transcendence, drawing her closer to the center of the void. Then the presence of another outside force took hold of her, drawing her back.

"Les. Les!"

She could faintly hear her name interspersed in the raucous tumult.

"Les!" Elliot sat in the chair next to Lesley nudging her and calling her name, not wanting to be too aggressive and possibly interfere with what might be a partial psychic seizure. Pulling her away too abruptly could adversely affect her complete recovery from the episode or cause a secondary, complex seizure. He grabbed an ophthalmoscope from his desk drawer and examined Lesley's eyes. The pupils reacted to the light, so he could assume no external chemical interference..

As Lesley's vision slowly returned, she barely made out a blurred face as she reacted with a soft hiss of a word. Was it really . . .

"Dad?"

"It's Elliot, Les."

She groggily stirred.

He helped her sit up. "Are you okay?"

"I think so." Trying to sit up, she fell back into the chair.

"Just relax."

Lesley couldn't do anything but relax.

"How long have you had this fever?" Elliot could feel the heat emanating from Lesley even from several feet away.

"I don't have a fever. At least I haven't had one." Lesley could now sit up on her own without feeling dizzy.

"What happened?" Elliot wet a towel with some bottled water and held it against Lesley's forehead.

"I don't know. I was just sitting here relaxing, waiting for you, and then drifted off into . . ."

"Have you been having any other symptoms lately, like -_"

"Elliot, I'm okay, really."

"You called me "Dad" when you were coming around."

Lesley didn't remember anything beyond just coming into Elliot's office and sitting in the chair. But to call out for "Dad"? Several years had passed since she last saw Arthur, and that meeting had not been under the best of circumstances.

"Have you seen him since the funeral?"

"No. And I don't want to talk about that."

"Look, Les, I know the past couple of years you've been pouring yourself into your work in an effort to not think about the accident. I haven't wanted to say anything, until now."

"Is that why you wanted to see me today?" Lesley could feel herself withdrawing into her shell like a crab escaping a predator.

"No, that's not why. But it's time you faced the fact that Conrad and your mother are gone, and nothing you can do will bring them back. And their accident wasn't anything you could have prevented. Lesley, this is starting to affect you physically, and it's not going to get any better until you do something about it."

Lesley didn't want to hear where Elliot was going with this. She removed the towel from her forehead and sat up.

"Why did you want to see me?"

"I really had two reasons. And I don't think you're going to like either one of them."

"If this is one of those good news/bad news things, just give me the bad first."

"No, it's nothing like that. I just wanted to talk to you about work mainly."

"Work has been just fine." Lesley couldn't think of any problems she was having with her teaching duties or research projects.

"I know that. It's not the quality of your work. You're a fabulous teacher, one of our best, and your research has been very productive. No, it's the amount of work. You're overloading yourself. This episode today is just the beginning of your body's reaction to it. I want to see you cut back, maybe even take a sabbatical. I can't even remember the last time you asked for a day off."

"Elliot, I can't just drop my research--"

"I'm not asking Lesley. I'm telling you, not just as the dean of the division, but as your Godfather and your friend and someone who cares for you very much. And for yourself. I want you to take some time off."

Lesley's mind raced now with all of the loose ends she would have to tie up if Elliot was really serious about making her take time off from her work.

"We only have a few weeks left of this quarter. You've trained your Grad Assistants very well. They'll be able to handle the classes for you."

"But the research on LGI1 needs to continue." Lesley felt desperation creeping in.

"LGI1 can wait a few weeks. We're not shutting it down. We'll give your team some time to begin writing up your findings and preparing your paper for the ACE meeting this summer."

"But, I --." Lesley couldn't handle the fact that she wouldn't be busy, immersed in an activity.

"Good. That's settled." Elliot wasn't going to hear any more pleas from Lesley. "Now for the next item. And I know you may not want to hear this."

Lesley guessed that it had to be better than what she had just heard.

"Arthur is in town. I figured that you didn't know."

And she didn't really care to know.

"He's guest lecturing at NYU tomorrow evening." Elliot let that sink in.

"Have you talked to him?" Lesley wasn't sure if she was ready for a discussion about Arthur yet.

"No. I just thought it might be time for you and him to clear the air. You two used to be so close. He couldn't move without tripping over you."

Lesley could see the images in her mind of following Arthur around campus, of him picking her up and carrying her when she couldn't keep up, of him standing in front of a class lecturing while she sat in one of the seats drawing, watching the students totally engaged in Arthur's lecture.

"Maybe he doesn't want to see me."

"Les, I know that a lot has happened to come between you two. But I also know Arthur, and I know how much he loves you. And, I would bet that he's being just as bull-headed about this as you are. I feel pretty sure that if you presented the opportunity for the two of you to talk that he would be willing."

"It's more than just being bull-headed, Elliot. I've been seeing someone, trying to work through the mess for over a year now."

"I'm very glad to hear that, Les." He leaned over and felt her forehead. "You're feeling cooler now. Are you still dizzy?"

"I'm okay."

"Good. Then you are now officially on sabbatical. We'll think of something for the paperwork in a day or two. You just go home and rest, and we'll talk in a few days. Why don't you get Jonathan to take you to Arthur's talk tomorrow night?"

That was another story all in itself. Another one Lesley didn't want to get into right then.

"I think he's busy tomorrow, but I haven't decided if I'm going yet."

"Well think about it."

"Of course." Lesley gave Elliot a hug and started for the door.

"Remember, no classes or research till you hear from me."

She nodded and left, saying "Good-bye" to Marta on her way through the outer office. She knew Elliot meant well, but she didn't know if she was ready to tackle seeing Arthur at this point. Maybe she would just go and stay to the back of the room and not let him see her. She would need to discuss today's incident with Lisa at her next session.

****

Lesley didn't need to stop by her office before she caught the metro to her co-op, only a short ride from the university in Washington Heights. She'd lucked upon the town home in Hudson View Gardens while living in the dorm in Bard Hall, where she had also met Jonathan. The grad assistant, Riley, who had leased the town home before her, had graduated and gone to Berkeley to complete his PhD and had been very friendly to Lesley. She had always suspected that he wanted to ask her out but was just too shy to follow through with the question, even though she had allowed him plenty of opportunities. So, when he left, he told her about the place and let her take over the remainder of his lease, which had already been paid through its term. Jonathan had always suspected something had gone on between the two of them, leading Lesley to think that he had possibly had something to do with Riley never asking her out.

Jonathan had insinuated himself into Lesley's life while she dealt with the death of her mother and brother. The loss of her brother and Arthur's conspicuous absence from the funeral, removed the two predominant male influences from her life, and she needed a male presence. Beyond the physical attraction that connected them, though, Lesley had little else in common with Jonathan. He'd been working as a teaching fellow in the PhD program in the Art History

Department and only needed to complete and defend his dissertation and would become a full faculty member the next year. His whole focus revolved around the world of art and aesthetics while Lesley's world revolved around science and medical research.

Lesley loved her town home. Each time she opened the door and stepped into the front room with its wall of windows looking out onto the Hudson, she immediately felt the calming character of the water flowing into her, and all the stress of the day disappeared. She couldn't imagine not living there and had repeatedly avoided Jonathan's pleas for her to move in with him and "save money." His apartment, though nice, was not at all as comforting to her, with its lack of windows and "art museum" feel.

Lesley dropped her bag on the floor, kicked off her pumps, poured a glass of Malbec, and plopped on the couch. It had been years since she had been in the position of not knowing what she would be doing for the foreseeable future, and she felt uncomfortable. No. She was really a little angry with Elliot for springing this on her so suddenly. She'd never really thought of a sabbatical before, even when she was in the early stages of working on LGI1. She really had no hobbies or pursuits outside of work.

The buzzing of her cell phone broke Lesley's train of thought. She didn't want to talk with anyone right now, especially not about anything important. She glanced at the screen and saw that it was Jonathan. Not now! Had he heard about her meeting with Elliot? Elliot had always thought she and Jonathan made a good couple and might have told him that she would be taking a much needed sabbatical. Jonathan would surely want to get together with her and remind her that he had been telling her the same thing for over a year and would probably have some suggestions for how she should spend her new free time.

She silenced the phone and tossed it aside. All she wanted was to relax and pour another glass of the Malbec. The next glass of Malbec did the trick. Lesley felt the exhaustion of the day close in. She stretched out on the couch, pulled up the comforter over her, and gave in to the calmness that filled the room.

****

The thunderclap shook the windows and startled Lesley awake. A storm had brewed while she slept, drenching the city for as far as she could see. She grabbed her phone to check the time. Shit. She'd left it on, and now the battery had run down. She didn't feel like getting up to find the charger. What did it matter anyway? She had nowhere she had to be and nothing she had to do. The only thing she really needed to do was think of something to do. She thought about how ironic that sounded. Normally she wouldn't even have time to lie on her couch for an entire evening and just relax. Now it was -- what time was it? The clouds hid any sunlight that might be showing, but she guessed that it was early morning by the traffic on the Hudson Parkway. At least she wouldn't have to get out in that today.

Lesley laid back onto the cushion and pulled the comforter up over her. Now that she was awake, the thoughts just started racing through her mind. But the one thought that kept popping out over the others was the thought of Arthur being in town. She agonized over the different scenarios of their meeting. Would he simply turn away and not even acknowledge her presence? Would they both share an awkward moment of silence and an even more awkward conversation afterward? Would they both admit the bull-headed way they had avoided each other for years and finally reconcile their past and hug each other to death? She could imagine forever and would never be able to predict the way the meeting would turn out. The only way to know would be to go to the talk and see what happened. The knock at the door surprised Lesley. Who could that be? Or maybe who else could that be?

All Lesley could see through the security viewer in the door was another eye peering back, but she knew who stood on the other side. She opened the door.

"I've been trying to get you since last night. Didn't you get my calls? My texts?" Jonathan squeezed through the doorway into the room. He could be very persistent.

"I forgot to charge my cell." Where was that charger?

Jonathan followed her into the room and closed the door behind him.

"Did you go out already or did you leave the door unlocked too?"

"I fell asleep on the couch." She'd better change the subject quick. "What are you doing up and around so early?"

"Early? It's almost eight o'clock. And why aren't you getting ready for work?" Apparently he hadn't heard yet. Better get some coffee going.

"I'm officially on sabbatical starting today."

"What? Wait a minute, let me sit for the rest of this." He slipped into a stool at the breakfast bar.

"No, I didn't have a sudden flash of logic and decide to do this on my own." Was that a smirk she almost saw. "Elliot insisted."

"Well, finally. Good for him." He got up from the chair and trapped her against the counter, his arms encircling her. "Can I suggest a few ways we can spend this time?"

His kiss caught her off guard and caused her to react coldly, but she soon warmed to him and let herself be kissed. This was a Jonathan she hadn't seen for a long while, the Jonathan to whom she had initially been attracted, the one who had provided the strength upon which she had relied when Conrad and Arthur had disappeared from her life. Or had she just gotten so involved in her work that she forced Jonathan to become someone else? Would this kiss last forever? She managed to release herself from the kiss.

"Don't you have a class to teach?" What she needed was a cup of coffee. She disentangled herself and reached for coffee cups.

"I'm thinking I need a sabbatical too. We can sabbatical together." He seemed pleased with this idea.

"I haven't really decided what I'm going to do yet. Elliot mentioned that Arthur will be giving a talk tonight at NYU. I was thinking about going there for a start." She sipped the coffee. Just strong enough.

"Wow. That's news. I finally get to meet the esteemed professor." That really wasn't what she wanted to hear.

"I had thought I might go this one alone. It's been so long, and I don't know how it's going to turn out. Maybe a disaster."

Disappointment peeked from behind Jonathan's smile.

"If it does go well, you'll have plenty of chances to meet him." Didn't seem to help.

Jonathan sipped the coffee, leaned against the counter. "I know this meeting has been on your mind for some time." He put his cup down and pulled her to him, taking her cup from her hand and placing it on the counter. "Just know that whatever way it turns out, I'll be waiting for you."

This time she was ready for his kiss, lost herself in it. It was a different kiss. More from a place of love than from a place of lust. She knew that Jonathan loved her. He'd convinced her of that without being too overbearing about it, had even offered her an engagement ring which she had politely refused, saying she wasn't ready to make that kind of commitment yet. She just didn't know if she felt that strongly for him, didn't want to lead him on to thinking that it was mutual until she was sure. The kiss ended as gracefully as it had begun.

"I'd better get going. I'll text Art and ask him to get the class started." This time just a peck on the cheek. Lesley followed him to the door.

He stopped in the doorway and turned back. "Good luck this evening. Call me."

"I will."

"And lock this door."

She grinned and shut the door behind him. Now to find the charger and get that phone working.

****

The call from Elliot came at about four o'clock. Luckily, Lesley had found the charger after Jonathan left that morning and had fully charged the phone.

"Hey, Les. How's the first day of freedom going?"

"I don't feel so free yet. Maybe when I figure out what I'm doing." Did that make sense?

"If you need suggestions, let's talk. That's not why I called anyway. I was wondering if you had planned to go to Arthur's talk tonight."

"I was planning on it. Why?"

"Because I'm not sure it's going to happen. I was supposed to pick him up at the airport over an hour ago, but he wasn't on the flight, and I haven't heard anything from him."

"Arthur's never been that great about phone calls or keeping in touch." She didn't even know if he had a cell phone.

"But as long as I've known Arthur, I've never known him to duck out on a presentation and not at least let someone know." Elliot was right about that.

"Maybe he just got bumped to a later flight or something." Lesley knew Arthur had to have some logical reason for not being on that flight.

"I called his place and only got his answering machine, which doesn't mean a lot, and I'll keep checking with the airline to see if he did get a later flight. I'll let you know as soon as I hear something."

"Thanks, Elliot."

Lesley pocketed the phone and sat facing the bay window. The sun peeked through the clouds off and on, raising the humidity and making the day rather muggy. More rain was predicted for that night. The perfect ingredients for a typical New York summer evening. The only ingredient that would make the evening more perfect would be finally getting back together with her father. But, after Elliot's call, she felt skeptical of the likelihood of that happening.

3

táá'

****

Sheriff Logan Branshee turned the key one more time in the ignition of his Bronco. Damnit! Another good deal from Big George Nakai that he'd have to take back. He popped the hood of the Bronco and checked the battery cables. Maybe Big George hadn't tightened the fittings tight enough. Big George was always in a hurry, moving on to the next customer with the next great deal. No. They were tight. He'd call Jay Littlefoot and have him stop by on his way into the office and get a jump from him. Then he'd find Big George and get another battery or get his money back and just go to Brown's Trading Post and spend the extra thirty dollars for a new battery. The dry heat and hot winds did a number on batteries in this climate, but Big George had given his "guarantee" that this one was the heaviest duty battery he had. He knew Big George got his name from telling tall tales, but usually you could trust him and would get a good deal. If the county would only give the Sheriff's office more of a budget to run its operations, he wouldn't be having these problems right now.

While he waited for Jay Littlefoot, he glanced through the messages that Darlene had brought to him. Even on his day off he could count on her to get his messages to him. Most were the usual. A kid bitten by a dog. Coyotes killing chickens. Fender bender on the 160 in town. Marge Dixon shot herself in the foot (he told her to be careful cleaning her gun!). Then a message from the Coyote Canyon Archaeological Research Center caught his attention. Dr. Whitney, he just called him "Doc," and the Doc didn't seem to mind, that professor who was doing research through the center, had not reported back from a field excursion deep into the Lost Canyon area. Usually the Bilagannas came in in their pressed Chinos and denim work shirts and three hundred dollar hiking boots and rented Range Rovers to go out into some of the roughest landscape in the whole country. And when they got lost or bottomed out, they wanted Branshee to come and rescue them. But the Doc was different.

Doc Whitney wasn't your average Bilaganna. He'd been coming to the area for years, even before Branshee had become Sheriff twelve years earlier, and he even had a little hogan outside of town. He'd been mapping Kivas and burial sites all over the area and had helped the center find some of its more important early Puebloan sites. He'd even heard that the Doc had been spending a lot of time with a Hopi Sorceress, Pine Leaf, learning some of the rituals and ceremonies and the history of the clans. The Doc knew the country pretty well, so he must have been gone for quite a while for the center to be calling Branshee about him. Or maybe something else was going on. He'd call them when he got to the office, if Jay Littlefoot would ever get there.

****

Branshee pulled into the pot-holed asphalt parking lot of his office about an hour later, cussing Jay Littlefoot under his breath. The Littlefoot clan held the honor of being the most laid back and unhurried people you'd ever meet, and contrary to their name, towered above most Navajo braves. Like in the case of Big George, who was not any taller than a Mesquite bush, lots of clan names had little to do with the actual person or were purposefully the opposite. Jay had gotten to him after picking up a goat from his grandfather to take to his uncle, who needed a male to court his female.

The morning sun had already baked the asphalt and made mirages of water puddles on the pavement. Darlene would have the office colder than a desert midnight in the dead of winter, not that he didn't like getting out of the heat, but he hated getting used to the cold and then having to go out on a call in the heat. He'd rather have the fans going with the windows open and sweat a little, but Darlene ran the office and had to be there all day. He'd heard on the radio that they might get some thundershowers in the afternoon up by Sleeping Ute Mountain. Maybe he'd need to take a stroll out that way to check on something later. Surely he could think of some reason to get out there.

"Mornin', Sheriff."

"Mornin', D. Don't say it."

"Why Sheriff, I wasn't gonna say 'must have been a big blow out last night at the Branshee place'."

"See if you can track down Big George and get him over here to look at that battery in my Bronco."

"Sure thing, Sheriff." Darlene could kid around like the best of them, but she was all business when it mattered.

Branshee rustled through the notes and papers on his desk and found the note from Coyote Canyon. He punched the number into his phone and got the front desk.

"Hello. This is Sheriff Branshee calling for Alan Hall."

"Let me see if Dr. Hall is in his office."

Branshee hadn't heard that name before. Must be new to the center.

"Hi, Sheriff, this is Alan Hall."

"Dr. Hall, I was calling about the message I received concerning Doc Whitney."

"Yeah, we're a little worried about him. He went up to the Lost Canyon area last week and was supposed to catch a flight to New York yesterday, but we haven't seen him or heard anything from him. He's not always the best for returning when he says he will, but he usually does at least check in with us every few days. And he wouldn't have missed his flight."

"How long was he planning on staying up there?"

"A couple of weeks. He's been doing a lot of work up there the past few months. Been pretty secretive about it."

"That's rough country." Branshee had been there lots of time and always took extra gear and supplies along, just in case.

"That's exactly why the director said I should give you a call."

"How is Barry. Haven't seen him in a while."

"Seems to be doing fine. You know, Sheriff, I know Arthur is a tough old guy, able to take care of himself and all, but anything could happen."

"Did the center send anyone to check on him?"

"We wouldn't even know where to look. And we're booked solid this week with students." The center's main income came from archaeological education programs for students in middle school and high school. That was how they funded their research work on the Puebloan peoples.

"All right. I won't file a missing persons report yet. I'll look into it and get back with you later on either this afternoon or in the morning."

"Thanks, Sheriff."

Darlene waved for Branshee's attention. "I've got Big George on the line."

"Tell him to get his butt down here. Now!" If he needed to go to Lost Canyon, Big George would be putting a new battery in his Bronco.

****

The drive from Cortez to Dolores on Highway 145 always calmed Branshee, no matter how badly his day was going, and he'd need to stay close to Dolores since Big George had only had a spare used battery to give him until he could get a new one. If he needed to go up into Lost Canyon after checking the Doc's hogan just south of Dolores on National Forest Highway 556, he'd have to wait for the new battery or just buy one in Dolores.

The Doc's hogan occupied a nice piece of land off the highway where the 556 crossed Lost Canyon Creek. The four acres lay lodged next to the creek, providing a goodly amount of water for growing vegetables or having a small garden, even for having a few chickens or a goat. Since the Doc went out for days or weeks at a time, he had someone come in to keep an eye on things for him, water the plants, feed the stock. He thought Billy Graywolf had been doing some of that but didn't know if he still was. Billy usually could be depended upon to do what he said, but he also took care of his grandpa, and that always came first to him.

The dirt road that led to the hogan, not much wider than a full-size pickup and filled with dips and mud puddles, especially after a rain, probably kept most unexpected visitors away from the place, so whoever was driving the Chevy pickup parked in the yard in front of the hogan must have had some reason to be out there. It wasn't Billy's. He drove his grandpa's old Ford F-100, and the Doc had one of those old Series 1 Land Rover's from England with the steering wheel on the right, probably the best vehicle for getting in and out of the terrain in that region. The Land Rover couldn't be seen anywhere around either. So, who was it paying the Doc a visit?

Branshee parked to the side of the front of the hogan, grabbed some extra rounds for his Colt Python, and stood beside the Bronco, following the tradition of waiting to be greeted and then invited into the home. He stood there surveying the area, looking for anything that appeared out of place or unusual. Nothing unusual stuck out, if his memory served him from the last time he'd been there. A couple of hens rested in the shade in the coup, hiding from the now fully risen sun. Some beans clung to the supports in the garden next to some tomatoes and peppers and yellow squash. Those along with some Navajo tacos would make a good meal pretty soon.

Nothing stirred from the hogan, so Branshee went to the front and peeked into the window. The darkness inside kept him from really being able to see anything, so he tried the door. It opened easily. He poked his head inside.

"Hello. Doc? Anybody here?" Again, nothing. But something didn't feel right.

He drew the Colt from its holster and stepped inside the door, patted the wall for a light switch. No lights. The Doc must have cut the power off while he was away. Branshee pulled his flashlight from his belt and scanned the room. He knew the Doc could be a little messy, but the mess the room was in had to have been done by someone looking for something. Desk drawers pulled out. Papers covering the floor. Furniture turned over with the undersides torn open. Probably whoever drove the Chevy out front. And that would mean they had to be around somewhere still.

Branshee hugged the wall, opened the shades to give him some more light. He could now see the extent of the disorder, but he really wanted to find the mystery guest who might be hiding somewhere in the room. Not many places to hide really. The hogan contained one big room with a kitchen area and a table, the living area with a desk and a couple of bookshelves, a door that led, he knew, to the bedroom and bathroom, and a door leading out the back. He checked the bedroom and bath. No one there. He'd come back later to take a closer look.

The back door opened to a several-acre yard area enclosed by Mesquite and Pinyon trees on both sides and a gradual slope leading down to Lost Canyon Creek. Again, not too many places to hide back there either. The Navajo Willow down by the creek had enough diameter to possibly hide someone, but they'd have to be pretty skinny to not be seen. The Doc's little skiff still rested by the creek, tied to the willow. Someone could lie down behind it and not be seen too well, but whoever it was, definitely had something particular they wanted. The artifacts on the shelves in the hogan hadn't been touched, so it most likely wouldn't be a looter looking to sell the artifacts to museums or private collectors. Anyway, those people usually would break into museums or research centers, like Coyote Canyon, or would dig artifacts from the sites that had just been opened or hadn't been completely excavated so they'd get enough to make it worth their while. No, this person had something specific in mind and wasn't going to waste time on anything else.

The water in the creek felt cooler than usual for that time of year. Branshee dipped his bandana in the water and wiped it across his forehead. That felt good. A bass splashed up the creek a ways. A good size fish. That would make some fine filets to go along with the vegetables in the garden. This was the kind of place he'd like to have in a few years when he put in for retirement. He already had his income from the military, twenty years and a couple of tours in Vietnam, and he'd be able to get his retirement from public service in another three. Those two together would more than take care of his needs. His wife had died of breast cancer eight years earlier, and their son had been killed during the Gulf War, one of the few casualties of that campaign. He couldn't even think of marrying again and preferred to just do his job and have a quiet, peaceful time in his retirement years, fishing and hunting and enjoying the outdoors.

The revving of the truck engine squashed Branshee's retirement dream. Damnit! He cocked the hammer on the Python and raced up the slope and across the yard, just in time to see the Chevy raising a cloud of dust speeding down the dirt road. If he'd really tried he could have probably caught the truck, if not for the front tires on his Bronco that were now flat. He'd have to call Dolores and get her to send Jay or Big George with another tire while he replaced one with his spare. He'd take a look around the hogan then while he waited and see what he could find out in there. Maybe he'd even have time to cool his feet in the creek, especially if he had to wait for Jay Littlefoot to get there. One thing for sure, he wouldn't forget that Chevy and would be keeping an eye out for it.

B. R. Fleming

4

di´i´'

****

The call from Sheriff Branshee had occupied Lesley's thoughts the entire morning.

"Is this Dr. Lesley Whitney?"

"Yes. I'm Dr. Whitney."

"Dr. Whitney, I'm Sheriff Branshee from Cortez, Colorado. I'm calling concerning your father."

Like anyone would, Lesley felt herself tense up and prepared for the worst possible news.

"I've been following up on a report we got from the research center your father works through here. They reported that they hadn't heard from the Doc -- sorry, that's what I call him --"

Lesley had to smile at that.

"-- since he'd headed up into Lost Canyon a couple of weeks ago."

"We were expecting him to be here for a talk at NYU a few nights ago too. Do you have any idea what's happened?" Lesley couldn't help feeling very lost and alone, thinking of the possibility that her entire family might be gone.

"All I know right now is that he went up into Lost Canyon on one of his field studies, nothing new for him, and hasn't been heard from since. One good thing is that he's not known for keeping in contact with the center."

"He's never been the best at keeping in touch at all." Branshee detected some resentment in Lesley's voice.

"That's pretty rough country, so we're hoping he hasn't had an accident or something worse. I'm going to be going that way today to scout around and see what I can find out."

"And what if you don't find anything?"

"The center didn't issue a Missing Persons Report yet, so a full-scale search hasn't been planned. And I really can't do anything more than what I'm doing without that. I can call you later and let you know what I do or don't find. Then, if you want to file the report, I can start a full-scale search for him, if need be."

Lesley didn't want to think about the "if need be" part. "Would I need to be there to file the report?"

"No. You could fax it to us or just tell me over the phone. Is this a good number to reach you at later?"

"Yes. But if I don't answer, just leave a message."

"Alright. Thanks, Ms. Whitney. I'll be back in touch."

It wasn't exactly the worst news Lesley could have gotten, but it could certainly have come at a better time. After all these years, she had finally been prepared to at least see Arthur at the talk, maybe to even talk with him. She hoped now that she would have another opportunity to do that. Had it been just bullheadedness that had kept her from opening channels with her father?

Since the accident with Conrad, she had felt responsible for the disconnection in her family that had resulted. Her mother had blamed herself for not going on the trip and had blamed Arthur for not watching out for her and Conrad. That had led to their eventual divorce. The fall had left Conrad paraplegic, but then he later developed epilepsy, most likely also related to the head injury suffered in his fall, since epilepsy had not appeared in any other members of their families for several generations. The guilt that Lesley had felt from Conrad's condition had been one of the instigating factors in her studies in Epidemiology but had led her to minimize contact with her family, except for with Conrad. In the back of her mind she had always felt that Arthur's limited visits after the divorce possibly stemmed from the same feeling of guilt. She found it difficult to face her mother, could see the pain in her expression every time they had to help Conrad into his bed or his wheelchair or into the van to take him to his physical therapy. Conrad tried to stay positive through it all, had even been taking classes in college, was on his way to class the day of the accident. Lesley had just begun her work on LGI1, had become absorbed in the work, so her mother had taken over the duty of driving Conrad in the van. Lesley always wondered if the same event would have occurred if she had been driving.

****

The flight from JFK to Denver had taken about four hours. Lesley hated to fly but accepted it as a logical means of transportation. While she waited for the shuttle that would take her to Durango, where she would rent a car to make the final leg of her trip to Cortez, she sat at the gate, sipped her chai latte, nibbled on the tuna sandwich she'd picked up at one of the food court snack bars. She had lost her appetite filing the Missing Person's report after speaking to Sheriff Branshee the second time and hearing the results of his trip to Lost Canyon.

"I found a campsite that could have been Doc's. It'd been pretty much torn apart by coyotes. No real clues around that would have linked it to him. No sign of the Land Rover either. I did find some tire tracks that could have been made by his Rover, though."

"Guess it's time to file the Missing Person's report. Right, Sheriff?" The reality of the situation hit Lesley.

"It's beginning to look that way."

After giving the Sheriff the information he needed, she called Elliot.

"I'm going to go out there."

"You sure you're up to that? I was hoping you would de-stress during your time off."

"I can't just sit around here and do nothing. At least if -- when they find him, I'll already be there."

Elliot agreed that she was right, and added, "Check in with the local CCID office, and I'll put in the paperwork for you to do some field study. That'll make your sabbatical legitimate."

Jonathan wasn't as agreeable.

"Les, you're not going to be able to do anything to help. I can see you now sitting around your room trying to find something to do stuck in the middle of nowhere."

"I know I won't be any help to them. I really thought you'd support me on this."

"You know I support you in whatever you decide." No comment. "Don't you? I just wish I could be there with you. I can't leave this class right now, and it'll be at least a couple of weeks before I can get out there."

"It should all be over by then, and I'll be back."

Lesley realized why she didn't like flying when the shuttle landed in Durango. The flight over the Rockies in the thirty-five-seater, turbo-prop, commuter had left a lot to be desired. Most of the passengers appeared okay with the constant bumping and bouncing of the plane on the wind currents over the mountains. About mid-way through the flight, Lesley began to wish she had never eaten the half of the tuna sandwich from the snack bar. After the plane came to a stop and everyone had disembarked, she collected her bags, rented a mid-size Audi sedan at the rental agency, got directions to Cortez, and started the hour-long ride on Highway 160, known as the Navajo Trail.

Lesley had little memory of the terrain of the area from her trip there with Arthur when she was younger, but she definitely remembered the smell and feel of the heat. It pierced her nostrils, dried the passageways down into her lungs, made her chest feel heavy, like it might collapse at any moment. Having an unrestricted view for miles and miles gave her a feeling of openness, too, that she never felt in the confines of the jungle of buildings that was New York City.

Just inside the city limits of Cortez, Lesley spotted a comfortable-looking motor hotel with an appropriate name for the area, the Turquoise Inn, pulled in, and registered. Her room was on the second floor, fairly secluded from the main traffic areas, offering a phenomenal view of Mesa Verde and Sleeping Ute Mountain. Gazing out of her window, she could understand why her father loved the area. The disparity between the towering pine and spruce tree-covered mountains and the rugged canyon lowlands produced an awe-inspiring landscape that begged to be explored, challenged, overcome. She could also understand why Arthur had chosen to study the Native Americans who had settled the region. He was just like them, one who invited those types of challenges, felt the exhilaration of exploring a land that questioned one's abilities, that constantly kept a person alive with the demands of living, of surviving.

She put her clothes away, set up her laptop, stored her luggage in the closet, and settled into the room, making it as comfortable as she could for a home away from home. The shuttle ride and the trip in the car had taken several hours and had sparked her appetite. She'd asked the desk clerk about local restaurants and had found out about a natural food market just up the street, several fast food restaurants within walking distance, and some family-owned restaurants in town. But she couldn't wait too long. As the desk clerk had mentioned, "They pull the streets in about nine around here. After that you'll have to settle for the 7-Eleven down at the junction." She'd gotten a room with a kitchenette, so she'd get some snacks and drinks at the natural foods market, call Sheriff Branshee and let him know she had gotten there, go to one of the restaurants the desk clerk suggested for dinner, let Elliot and Jonathan know she made it okay, and then settle in for the night. She'd had enough traveling and moving around for one day.

✳✳✳✳✳✳✳✳✳✳✳✳✳✳✳✳✳✳✳✳✳✳✳✳✳✳✳✳✳

The morning shower felt refreshing after spending the previous day travelling. Lesley finished brushing her long, fine, blondish-brown hair, touched up her makeup, the little that she wore, and straightened the bathroom counter. She took one last look in the mirror. The years had been good to her. She'd always kept herself in shape, worked out, ate healthily, tried to avoid over-indulging. The Mexican food the night before had hit the spot. Seafood enchiladas, Navajo rice, black beans, salsa and chips, not to mention the yummy Margaritas. A lot different from the Mexican food served in most New York City restaurants and seemed much fresher. Taking the Sheriff's advice over the suggestions of the desk clerk had proven to be a good decision. She'd nibble later on the chips and salsa and half of a seafood enchilada that didn't get eaten last night.

She checked the "to-do" list on her make-shift work table. Her first stop for the day, after getting her morning chai and a bagel or croissant, maybe she'd try some of the Navajo bread, was to meet the Sheriff and ride out to Arthur's hogan. Later that afternoon she planned to go to the research center and talk to the director and some of the people there about Arthur's work with them, find out where he might have been excavating the past few weeks. Sheriff Branshee had told her that they would probably be busy with students during the day and that the late afternoon might be better for talking with them. That would also give her and the Sheriff plenty of time to go through Arthur's papers and such at the hogan. Apparently, the place had been left in a mess, which didn't sound like Arthur.

The drive to the hogan was somewhat rougher than her drive from Durango the day before. The Sheriff had felt that her Audi wouldn't do well on the dirt road from the main highway to the hogan, so they had taken his Bronco, which seemed inclined to explore every bump and rut in the highway. And the dirt road promised to be even worse, but Lesley knew that she had better get used to the more rugged roads unless she planned on staying in her room the whole time she was there. Except for some light conversation and the faint background country music from the radio, the ride had been fairly quiet.

"What kind of doctor are you, Ms. Whitney?"

"I'm an Epidemiologist."

"So, let's see, you study diseases that could become epidemic if not kept under control. Like the flu, polio, smallpox?"

"Yes, basically that's one of the jobs of an epidemiologist. I particularly study the genetic factors involved in the transmitting of disease or abnormalities through heredity." After she said it, Lesley thought how clinical it sounded.

"Is that the dictionary definition?" A slight grin spread across Branshee's face.

"I'm sorry, Sheriff. I'm used to speaking to students and colleagues on campus."

"You don't get out much?"

"I've been pretty immersed in my work the past few years." Only Lesley knew that was a vast understatement.

"How long has it been since you saw your father?"

Lesley felt the flush on her face.

"Didn't mean to get too personal. You just stated that your father wasn't too good at keeping in touch, so I figured you might not have seen him for a while."

"We had a falling out." Lesley paused, stared out the window. "I've actually been here before, Sheriff. When I was younger. With my father." Another pause. "And my brother."

Branshee sensed Lesley's discomfort with the subject. "Then you're well aware of the heat and dryness in this area, I would imagine. Make sure you take plenty of water with you anywhere you go."

Lesley smiled a "Thank you" smile. "I will." She dug around in the bag she had brought and pulled out her water bottle, held it up to show Branshee.

He grinned. Not quite what he had implied, but at least she had thought to bring some.

They arrived at the hogan and found Billy Graywolf getting ready to leave on a Yamaha dirt bike. He had just settled onto the seat when he spotted the Sheriff's Bronco, shut off the engine, and stood next to the bike, waiting for the Sheriff to get out.

"Yá'át'ééh, Billy."

"Yá'át'ééh."

"I'll be right back." The Sheriff walked over to Billy, talked with him in Navajo.

Lesley took a few minutes to scan the area. It looked like exactly the kind of place where she could picture Arthur living. Simple. Only the essentials. Not a lot to have to keep up. The chickens. The vegetable garden. Plenty of water. Did she hear a goat in back? She walked across the yard and around the side of the house and spotted a boat in the shade of one of the trees down by the creek. Arthur had always been partial to fishing when not working and had taken Lesley and Conrad with him sometimes when he went. Arthur didn't believe in a heavenly realm, but if he had, this is what heaven would be for him.

Lesley heard the motorcycle starting and peeked around to the front yard to see Billy zooming off and Sheriff Branshee walking toward her.

"Billy's been keeping the place up for the Doc. Says he hasn't seen anyone around since the Doc took off. He doesn't go in the house. Just takes care of the stock and the garden. Let's go in."

Lesley followed Branshee into the hogan and immediately felt a shiver resonate up and down her spine, the darkness of the room intensifying the aura of menace that seemed to seep from the walls. This was not Arthur's doing. Something or someone else had been here and had left the disarray, had left behind a sentinel to keep watch. But for what?

"This is exactly the way I found it the last time." The Sheriff scanned the room with his flashlight, highlighting the overturned furniture, the papers strewn about, the books and artifacts on the shelves, obviously out of place.

"Haven't had a chance to get the electricity going." Branshee opened the shade on one of the windows, then opened the other shade, then went to the back door and opened it.

A sudden gust of wind rushed past Lesley, knocking her down, causing a swirl of dust in the middle of the room and forcing Branshee out through the back door. The wind intensified, sounding and feeling like a tornado passing through, as Branshee fought to get back in. Lesley lay on the floor trying to get up but could only raise up on one elbow, the wind and dust holding her in place like a net. The more she struggled to get up, the more the net tightened its hold on her. Surprisingly, faintly, through the roar of the wind, a slow rhythmic thumping captured Lesley's attention, like a heartbeat, gradually beating louder and louder. She searched through the fog of dust for Branshee and caught a glimpse of a form in the center of the maelstrom, a hump-backed figure more insect-like than human, writhing in time to the rhythm of the thumping. Fear overcame Lesley. She screamed for Branshee.

"Sheriff!" He probably wouldn't be able to hear her screams through the din accompanying the storm invading the room. "Sheriff!" It was useless. She collapsed onto the floor.

Branshee had managed to work himself back into the room but had been glued to the wall by the force of the storm. He couldn't see Lesley but knew that she had to be somewhere within the hogan, hopefully unharmed. Then, as suddenly as the wind had commenced, it abruptly stopped. The dust remained, clinging to the air, clouding Branshee's search for Lesley. He called to her.

"Doctor Whitney?" He heard a moan. He could just make out a mound of something on the floor in the middle of the room. Branshee waded through the thick cloud to the center of the room and reached down to grab Lesley and pull her up to him and then made his way to the back door. He placed Lesley on the grass outside the door and went to his truck to grab a blanket. When he returned, Lesley had sat up and rested her back against the hogan wall, brushing the dust off. She coughed and sneezed from the dust that had settled in her throat and lungs.

"Good. You're up." He knelt beside her and gave her the blanket.

"What was that?" Lesley took the blanket and put it behind her head.

"Normally, I'd say we just experienced a Dust Devil. But that one came and went pretty quickly." He didn't want to tell her what he really thought. At least, not yet. "You okay."

"I'll be fine in just a minute." The coughing wasn't so bad now. "I saw something in the dust."

"What?"

"I'm not sure what it was. It looked like a big insect. It was holding onto a stick or something, and it looked like it was dancing."

"That sounds pretty strange alright. Probably just the light playing tricks with all the dust and stuff blowing around." Or . . .

"Can we still have a look in the hogan?"

Branshee peered through the back door and saw that the dust had almost completely settled or been blown out by the slight breeze the storm had left behind.

"Almost clear enough to get in there."

Lesley stood up and followed Branshee just inside the door. Except for the thin film of dust still clinging to the air, the room looked pretty much the same as when they had first opened the door. Lesley stepped into the room and began gathering papers from the floor, stacking them on the work table. Whoever had been here was after something in particular, something not necessarily valuable to anyone else. Had they found it? Arthur always kept a journal of the digs, but she hadn't found anything like that yet. He would probably have that with him anyway. Was that what the intruder was after?

Branshee made mental notes of the room, the displacement of the furniture, the undisturbed artifacts on the shelves. Why would someone tear through the furniture and then not touch the items on the shelves?

"Do you know what your father was working on, Ms. Whitney?"

"You would probably know more about that than I would. Like I said, we haven't really talked that much lately. And these papers look pretty general. Some maps, notes. I'll have to go through them."

"I didn't get much from the center either. Just that he spent a lot of time in Lost Canyon."

"Dad was always pretty secretive about his work. He wanted to have all the questions answered before he published or made any predictions. He didn't like loose ends or for someone to ask a question that he couldn't answer." She found a messenger bag and began stuffing it with the papers, notes, and maps. "What's so special about Lost Canyon?"

"It's a good sized canyon but pretty much like the other canyons in these parts. Just more remote and more rugged a terrain. Even the center hasn't done any work in that area. Used to be some mining going on up there. The railroad ran a line through there, but they shut it down when the mining stopped. Nobody hardly goes up there anymore. Just people like your dad. The occasional prospector."

"People like my dad meaning nut cases?"

"Well, you kind of have to be nuts to be going up there for any length of time. No, that's not what I meant. Exactly." They both grinned at this.

"I'm not really finding much here, Sheriff. But I'll take these papers and go through them. I'm going to the center later on this afternoon and talk with one of the instructors there, Alan Hall. Maybe he'll know more about what dad's been doing."

"Yeah, I talked with him when they reported the Doc missing. Didn't seem to know much, but it would probably be good for you to talk with him anyway. Introduce yourself. I'll get Jay Littlefoot to keep an eye on this place. If whoever came before comes back, we'll be ready for them."

5

'ashdla'

****

Alan Hall coached his favorite cedar rocking chair in time with the haunting rhythm of the drum accompanying David Nighteagle's flute playing. The rocking chairs held a position of prestige on the porch of the lodge, filling up quickly with the teachers and chaperones from the visiting school groups and with any center instructors during breakfast or lunch breaks or who happened to be on campus for an evening activity. The lodge deck proved the perfect setting for this evenings' activity, David Nighteagle's presentation of Native American flute-making and his performance of his own flute songs, which ranked as one of Alan's favorites chaperone activities.

The sun had already crept behind the hills but still revealed Coyote Canyon and the surrounding mountains of the San Juan National Forest and Mesa Verde. He watched the students gathered on the deck as they squirmed in anticipation of having the evening free for other fun activities but knew that David had, as always, kept their attention with his jokes and by getting the students involved in playing his array of percussion instruments, while introducing them to the Native American flute and its spiritual presence in Native American life. Afterwards, they would gather around him to buy his exquisitely hand-crafted flutes to show off to their friends and would purchase the cd's of his flute music to remind them of their last night on campus.

Alan had another reason to stay on campus that evening. He had gotten a message that the daughter of Arthur Whitney, Lesley he thought, wanted to talk with him about her father's work with the center. He wished that he had talked with her and could have told her himself that he didn't really know much about Arthur's work and could have saved them both a little time. He had only met with Arthur a couple of times and hadn't really had much opportunity to sit down and talk with him about his work. He knew of Arthur's reputation as an expert in Native American spiritualism and ancient peoples, everyone on the center staff was aware of that, but that was about as far as their connection went.

The applause at the end of David's flute piece signaled Alan it was time to gather the troops. He reluctantly pried himself from his post and made his way through the students to David and grabbed one of the microphones.

"This has really been a special treat, right students." More applause from the teachers and students. "David, thank you for a very special evening." David had already begun gathering his equipment with the help of his drummer and girlfriend, Marianna, and was readying to sell his wares but stopped to wave acknowledgment of the thanks.

"If you wish to purchase flutes or cd's, please line up at the table over at the right of the stage. David and Marianna will be there in a moment to help you. And don't forget that tonight you need to pack and be ready in the morning to board the bus to take you to Albuquerque.”

Students leapt to their feet and began scattering into the lodge to play games or watch DVD’s or begin packing. Others flocked to the field in front of the center to let off some pent up energy from sitting for so long or gathered with their teachers at David’s table to spend the last of their trip allowance on souvenirs.

Alan made his way back through the crowd to the rocking chairs, shooed away one of the students, and nestled into the chair and resumed the unhurried cadence, now to a rhythm that occupied his thoughts. A vehicle coming toward the lodge in a rather reluctant manner grabbed his attention. He hoped that this was finally Arthur’s daughter getting there. He wanted to get home to his condo and change clothes and grab a bite to eat before it got too late, and he didn’t expect that it would take too long to brief her on what he knew.

The Audi stopped in the parking area, and a woman emerged from the driver’s side. So far, so good. Alan could taste the tamales from Mama Rosa’s already. Fresh made every day with cheese and chile or cheese and chicken or just about anything you’d want in a tamale. As the woman approached the deck, Alan couldn’t help but notice how pretty she was. Her long brown hair clung to her shoulders and mirrored her slender figure. She stopped to talk with one of the chaperones who pointed toward Alan on the porch. Alan tried to not be too obvious in his staring at her.

She stepped onto the porch and held our her hand. “Hi. I’m Lesley Whitney.”

“I’m pleased to meet you, Ms. Whitney. I’m Alan Hall.” Her soft hand proved that she worked in Academia. He shooed away another student in the chair next to him and offered it to her.

"Thank you for meeting with me. I hoped that I could get a better idea of what my dad was doing out here." She looked uncomfortable sitting in the chair. Apparently she had never had a meeting in a rocking chair before.

"Would you rather go inside to one of the tables?"

"No. This is fine." She sat back in the chair and gently began rocking. Her eyes closed, and the rocking became steady, rhythmic.

Alan watched her. She had lovely features, graceful cheekbones, nicely contoured lips. Her hair swayed with the rocking and brushed against her ample breasts.

"How do you get any work done around here?" She smiled now.

"Oh, we manage." They both laughed.

"Arthur used to love to sit here in the evenings whenever he came out. You know, I knew Arthur before coming here."

"Oh, yeah."

"Yeah. He was a visiting professor in Austin while I was there at the university. Pretty much solidified my intent on becoming an archaeologist after going through his workshops and hearing him talk about his experiences."

"He had that effect on people quite often."

"I also have to tell you that I'm not going to be much help for you. I don't really know that much about Arthur's work here. Nobody does. He discovered some of the sites I've worked and the one I'm excavating now. But he kept to himself and didn't really share much of what he was doing up in Lost Canyon. He had independent funding, so he didn't really have to report anything to the center. He simply used the center as a base of operations."

"Why Lost Canyon?"

"It's one of the most inaccessible canyons to the average hiker or visitor to the region. Mostly prospectors and railroad people go up there, and they aren't really looking for archaeological sites. It's rough country. You need a 4-wheel drive or a horse to get in and out easily. If any sites existed up there, they'd probably be fairly untouched."

"That's pretty much what Sheriff Branshee said too. It certainly sounds like the kind of place dad would be exploring. He always gravitated to the most remote areas. Why hasn't the center done any exploration in that area?"

"Money, mainly. We depend a lot on students and volunteers to do much of the real excavation work. It's just not the kind of place where we'd want to take young students. Besides, the area here around us has so many sites that we could spend the next hundred years just digging on this side of the San Juan Mountains."

"Would you mind taking a look at some papers that we found at dad's hogan? I couldn't make much out of them, but maybe you could." Lesley suddenly looked despondent.

"What exactly do you hope to find, Lesley? I'm sure the Sheriff will do everything he can to find out what happened to Arthur or where he is."

"Tell you the truth, I don't really know. I'm just kind of going through the motions these days."

"Hey, have you eaten yet?"

"No. I came straight here from the Sheriff's office after we left dad's hogan."

"Well, I planned to go to Mama Rosa's tonight to have some of the best tamales ever made. If you want, you could join me, and we could take a look at your dad's papers."

"I could really go for a salad tonight. I had enchiladas last night."

"I'm sure Mama can get a wonderful salad together for you. But you have to at least have a bite of the tamales. You won't regret it."

"Alright. I'd like to go to my room and change first, if that's okay."

"Sure. I'll pick you up there in about an hour."

****

Mama Rosa's cantina lay well off the beaten path outside of town heading toward Sleeping Ute Mountain. The place looked like an abandoned adobe-style train stop from the outside, occupying a corner next to the railroad line at a railroad crossing. Even the trucks and worn out vehicles lining the front of the building looked like they'd been gathering dust there for ages. On first glance, Lesley thought that she would have never dreamed of going there if Alan hadn't taken her.

The main dining area inside, though, presented a completely opposite, welcoming atmosphere. Chiles hung from the posts and ceiling like stalactites; a circular fountain graced the center of the room producing a peaceful, waterfall background sound; planters filled with succulents and ferns divided the room into different sections; the lighting seemed to emanate from inside the walls themselves. Cozy without being elaborate.

Lesley wandered around the menu but couldn't really make much out of it as it was mostly in Navajo. She hadn't eaten anything of substance since breakfast and could feel her blood sugar starting to react. A piece of the Navajo flat bread the waitress had brought would help until the meal came.

"What do you suggest? This was your idea." The salad still sounded good. "Remember, I had Mexican last night."

"Hate to tell you this, but that was nothing more than Bilaganna, Americanized southwestern food."

"Bilaganna?" Lesley didn't care. Tasted yummy to her.

"White people." Alan returned his attention to the menu. "The tamales can't be beat, and you can get just about anything you want in them or on the side. Cheese. Beef. Chicken. Rattlesnake. Desert hare. Or my favorite, the blue corn cactus and chile tamale with gazoo cheese. That's cheese made from the yucca plant. This is very traditional Navajo fare. Lots of corn, veggies, beans, the Three Sisters. Even the fry bread is made with a mixture of corn and wheat flour and with juniper ash instead of baking soda."

"Okay. I'll take your word for it. You decide."

"Let's just get a couple of entrees, some tamales and fry bread with some veggies and beans and just eat what you want of each. Sound good?"

"I'm game." Lesley took a bite of the fry bread.

"Oh, and a side salad too."

Alan ordered the meal from Mama Rosa herself, a slightly plump Navajo woman, with long shiny black hair who made several glances in Lesley's direction as if sizing her up. Lesley grabbed the messenger bag and showed it to Alan.

"We found these papers at Dad's hogan today. The place had been ransacked. Someone was looking for something in particular."

"Why do you think that?"

"Some artifacts were still on the shelves. Some mugs, some storage vessels. The Sheriff said that looters would have probably taken those."

"Probably. We have quite a problem around here with artifact hunters. We try the best we can, and so do the Navajo authorities, to keep the sites secure. Just too many sites and too much in them to attract the scavengers."

Alan glanced through the papers. "This is pretty general stuff. I don't see anything unusual or very specific."

"Neither did I. But I wouldn't know exactly what to look for either. I do know that Dad had a notebook that he kept with him at all times. He would never even let us look at it."

"I assume you didn't find one at his hogan." Their drinks came. "I hope you like the Navajo beer. We can order something else if it's too strong for you."

"I'm not much of a beer drinker. I could go for a Margarita, though, and you can have the beers." Lesley took a sip of the beer, winced, and slid it over to Alan. "No. To answer your question. We didn't find a notebook or any more personal stuff at the hogan."

"So what's next?"

"The Sheriff issued a Missing Person Report and plans to go back to Lost Canyon with some more help and search again. I'm going to go to the CCID office in Durango and check in."

Alan's quizzical look told Lesley that he had no idea what she meant.

"I'm on sabbatical from my work at Columbia. The Coordinating Center for Infectious Diseases is a branch of the CDC."

Now she had peeked Alan's interest. "What kind of work do you do at Columbia?"

"I do genetic research and teach."

"Sounds interesting."

"I love my work. Maybe a little too much. Anyway, I have to check in with the CCID as a part of the sabbatical. Boss' orders."

"You might want to talk to one of the instructors at the center while you're at it."

"Oh." Now Alan had peeked Lesley's interest.

"Her name is Shanee. She was friends with Arthur."

"Friends?" Lesley wondered just what that meant.

"Okay. I heard they were maybe a little more than friends, but I can't verify that. David Nighteagle might also be good to talk to. I know he was helping Arthur get in touch with a Navajo sorceress."

Lesley wondered just what Arthur was into now.

The meal came, and Lesley and Alan chit-chatted about nothing in particular throughout the remainder of the evening. But Lesley couldn't help but wonder what she might find out from Shanee and what kind of relationship she might have had with her father.

Alan had been right. Mama Rosa's tamales could pass even the most stringent tamale taste tests, though Lesley was no expert on the matter. They finished the meal, paid the bill, and thanked Mama Rosa for the delicious food.

"You bring this pretty lady back with you again, Mr. Alan." Mama Rosa smiled at Lesley. Apparently, Lesley had gained Mama Rosa's dinner date approval.

The now empty parking lot, except for a Chevy truck parked in the shadows, would have presented a challenge to find Alan's Jeep Cherokee had it not been for the presence of the full moon rising in the night sky. Lesley and Alan made their way to the Cherokee, got in, and took off. After a few moments, the Chevy truck followed.

About an hour later, following another round of chit-chat and getting gas for the next day, Alan dropped Lesley off at the Turquoise Inn. She felt his eyes follow her all the way inside and turned and waved as he took off. She sensed his attraction to her and couldn't deny her attraction to him, cute and interesting, but . . .

As she approached the steps to the second floor, the desk clerk caught her attention.

"Ms. Whitney. I have a some phone messages for you."

She checked her cell phone. Dead. She had forgotten to charge it that afternoon. Maybe she needed a new battery. She'd check around town the next day for a store.

The clerk handed her the messages. "Thank you." She immediately sifted through them.

Les. Tried to call. Think you need a new battery. I'll send one if you can't find one out there. Call when you get this. Love you. Jonathan

That one could wait until the morning.

Where are you. Been trying to reach you all afternoon. I miss you. Call me as soon as you get this message. Love you. Jonathan

Maybe she should call when she got to the room. What would she tell him about tonight?

Les. Hope you're relaxing and enjoying the time off. A package came to your office today, from Arthur. Thought you might want it out there, so I sent it to you UPS. Should be getting it in a day or two. Have you checked in with the CCID yet? Keep in touch. Elliot. P. S. Get your cell phone checked.

A package from dad? Why on earth after all this time would he be sending packages to her?

The room invited her to relax after her long day. Lesley slipped out of her clothes, took a quick shower, and readied for bed. She didn't really feel like going on the laptop, so she slipped into the over-sized bed and turned on the TV to catch up on the news.

Paid advertisements and shopping networks populated most of the channels. No wonder she didn't watch TV. But then a local news channel caught her attention. On the screen, a reporter stood in the foreground of a large group of Native Americans with the words Navajo Nation Rally on the bottom of the screen. Lesley turned up the sound.

" . . . and the full support of the Navajo Tribal Council. Earlier this evening, Bold Sun, the leader for the Navajo

Nation on matters concerning artifacts and preservation of lands, spoke to the gathering."

Now the face of a Native American man with long black hair pulled back in a ponytail and wearing a Navajo design headband filled the screen.

". . . and the desecration of these sites and the great Kiva, the way other sacred objects have been stolen and desecrated, is just another way for the Bilaganna and the government to dictate the lives of Native Americans!"

Applause, cheers in the background.

"We will fight to keep our sacred lands sacred, unspoiled by the Bilaganna!"

More cheers.

"We will fight to keep our heritage and resist the government's attempts to destroy our ancient way of life."

More cheering.

"And we will oppose any attempts by the government to educate and medicate our people into the white man's world."

The people begin a chant. "Chev-e-yo! Chev-e-yo! Chev-e-yo! Chev-e-yo!"

The newscaster returned to the screen with the chants still permeating the background.

"We'll see in the next few weeks what the next move will be by the Navajo Nation. This is Jennifer Logan, reporting from Montezuma County Courthouse in Cortez. Back to you Dana."

The speaker's last statement seemed rather curious to Lesley. She decided it really was time to get to sleep. Lesley turned the TV off and plugged her phone into the charger. Maybe charging the battery would fix what was wrong with the phone. Calling Jonathan should rank first on her to-do list for in the morning, to ease his mind. Then a call to the CDC regional office in Fort Collins and a visit to the center to talk with Shanee. When did Sheriff Branshee plan to go back to Lost Canyon? Maybe she should take a trip up there too.

All the thoughts now overwhelmed her. She wished that she could have brought some of the New York rain with her that always calmed her and helped her to sleep. She dug her mp3 player out of the bottom of her carryon bag and plugged it into the input on the radio. A little Ralph Towner would work almost as well as the rain. Before the first tune had ended, she had drifted off to sleep.

In the parking lot, a Chevy truck slowly passed in front of the Inn, stopped momentarily, then sped out of the driveway onto Highway 160, disappearing into the night.

The Secret People

6

hasta´a´

****

The sun caressed the canyon walls, rays bouncing from side to side, intensifying on each pass till, by the time the beams reached Branshee, the canyon floor felt like Running Foot's sweat lodge. The teams had scoured the canyon and the outcrops for twenty miles and could find no trace of Arthur Whitney. Branshee still wondered if the camp he found belonged to the Doc. He hadn't really found evidence of the Doc being there, and the tire tracks didn't belong to the Doc's Rover. Had the Doc even been here? One of the teams emerged from an outcrop and strolled toward the Sheriff.

"Anything?" Branshee already knew the answer he'd get from Jay Littlefoot.

"Ky-ote tracks; coupla rattlers; some donkey dung. Nothin' human."

The men collapsed against the rocks and emptied canteens over their heads, into their too dry mouths.

"Tell ya' one thing, no human's been there for a while. Bet the south team finds the same."

"Yeah. Figured that'd be what we found. Get your men and get back to town. I'll wait for the other team."

"Hágoónee'."

"Lá'aa, hágoónee'."

Branshee watched as the team piled in the Ram and headed out of the canyon. What else could he do? If someone didn't want to be found, Branshee'd have a tough time trying to find him. Though the team had now travelled out of sight, he didn't feel alone. One of those itches that can't be scratched gnawed at him. How had the team missed that? Jay Littlefoot didn't make those kind of mistakes. Could be the heat had played tricks on him. Without the Python he'd have to act as calm and cool as possible.

About two hundred yards up the canyon, movement caught his eye. Not much he could do at this point. Get back to the Bronco. Get the Python. Radio the South Team. He splashed some water in his face, ambled to the Bronco. He leaned on the door, took a sip of the water, tossed the water bottle in the seat. He could reach the Python now if he needed. He'd have to get in to reach the radio.

He wouldn't need that after all. He could hear the south team coming up the canyon floor. Hadn't seen any more movement either. Even with binoculars, no life stirred within range. Maybe just his imagination. He'd get the team turned around and back to Cortez, figure out his next move.

✳✳✳✳✳✳✳✳✳✳✳✳✳✳✳✳✳✳✳✳✳✳✳✳✳✳✳✳✳

The cell phone worked great. Just needed a full night's charge. Lesley would check out getting a spare battery, just in case. If she did decide to go up to Lost Canyon, she'd need the phone. But would she even get reception out there?

The assistant director of the Communicable Disease Epidemiology Section of the state health department, which operated as part of the CDC national network, asked Lesley if she could help their offices with gathering data on native children that lived on the various native lands in the area. Their offices had been overtaxed with a flu outbreak in the Denver area and a helping hand would be appreciated. She was happy to help and said she'd have Elliot send the paperwork to verify she was actually doing some work for them in conjunction with her sabbatical. She could do some data collecting of her own that would tie in with her LGI1 research. She couldn't remember any data from native populations and could use the information when she returned to Columbia.

The entire morning, her thoughts had bounced from last night's outing with Alan to her coming meeting with Shanee. Talking with Jonathan had helped ease his mind that she was safe and sound and that she really didn't have anything to report.

"I'll come out if you want. I can have my GA cover my class for a week or two."

"I don't know if I'll even be here that much longer. You were right about not having much to do except sit around the room." Last night wouldn't get mentioned, she'd decided.

"See. I am right some times."

They had left the call at "let's see what's going on by the end of the week." Sheriff Branshee hadn't discovered anything more on his second search of the canyon and had reservations that the camp he'd found had even been Arthur's. He would keep the Missing Person Report on file and active and would continue to investigate every possible avenue for leads, but he confessed that he didn't have much else to check out. Did he know about Shanee? David Nighteagle? This sorceress Arthur had been seeking? Surely he would have talked with those people.

She reached the center a little after noon and had to weave her way around and through the groups of students playing games and hanging out around the lodge. The activity and energy of the students reminded her of the Columbia campus and made her feel a little homesick. What was she doing here? She needed to be back at school continuing her research, working with her students. This felt more and more like a waste of time. Sure, she wanted to know what had happened to Arthur, but that was going nowhere. This was just like him too. Disappear and have everyone wondering where he was and when, if, he was ever coming back.

The receptionist at the main building called for Shanee and said she'd be able to give Lesley a few minutes before she had to conduct a lab for the students. Lesley wandered around the lobby and the gift store, intrigued by the artifacts on display. The hallway to the offices, lined with maps of the various excavation sites the center had researched, especially caught her attention. She could just imagine Arthur being there, examining the finds, offering his advice, conferring with the local archaeologists and native peoples. No wonder he had spent over a quarter of his life there.

A tall, very pretty, blonde approached Lesley. She didn't really look like an archaeologist, but what were archaeologists supposed to look like?

"You're Lesley." She held out her hand. "You have Arthur's eyes."

She must have studied Arthur very closely. "Yes. Alan Hall mentioned that you knew my dad and that I should talk with you."

"Let's talk over here." Shanee led Lesley to a secluded area of the main room off the reception area. They settled into the Southwestern-styled chairs.

"What exactly did Alan tell you about Arthur and me?"

Lesley thought for a moment. She didn't want to blow Alan's confidence, but she wanted Shanee to be as honest as possible with her.

"He said that you and dad knew each other and that he'd heard that you were more than just friends."

Now Shanee thought for a moment.

"Arthur and I were very close. We spent a lot of time together, at the hogan, at my place. He didn't share much about his work with me, except that he was working with a Hopi sorceress named Pine Leaf."

"Do you know what he was doing in Lost Canyon?"

"He was most secretive about his work up there. I didn't even ask him about it, because I knew he would change the subject if I did."

"Do you know what he was doing with this Hopi woman?"

"Not exactly. But before he disappeared, if he even has, he was spending more and more time with her. He would even sometimes be gone for days at a time. That's one of the reasons why we didn't think it so unusual for him to be out of touch with us."

"You don't think he's missing?"

"Something has happened, but I think it was something intentional."

"Have you ever talked with Pine Leaf."

"No. But I know David Nighteagle was the one who hooked them up. When do you plan to go back to Columbia."

Lesley gave Shanee a quizzical look.

"Oh, I know a lot about you. Arthur talked about you quite a bit. He loves you very much and really regretted not being closer with you the last few years. That's one reason he had planned to do the talk at NYU. He hoped he'd get to see you."

Lesley felt an emptiness enter her stomach. Why had he been so elusive all these years? She decided she hadn't known him as well as she thought.

"I don't have a set date that I have to be back. I'm going to be doing some data collection for the CCID while I'm here, probably take a couple of weeks."

"You should definitely talk with David then, and try to get in touch with Pine Leaf." Shanee glanced at the clock on the wall. "I have to get ready for my lab. Maybe we can talk again, go to dinner or something."

"Yes, I'd like that." Lesley felt a connection to Shanee and could understand Arthur's attraction to her.

Shanee disappeared down the main steps. Now Lesley needed to try to find David Nighteagle.

✳✳✳✳✳✳✳✳✳✳✳✳✳✳✳✳✳✳✳✳✳✳✳✳✳✳✳✳

After stopping at the reception desk and getting directions, Lesley headed out to find David Nighteagle. She hadn't seen Alan while at the center. Wonder what he was doing today? Maybe she'd call him later.

The road to David's place took Lesley south of Cortez on Highway 160 and then west almost to Utah until she reached Highway 41. The roads kept getting narrower and more bumpy and worn down the farther she went. The terrain became wilder and more beautiful. Ute Peak rose in the distance to the east of her and to the west lay mostly desert-type, flat plain with outcrops of mountains in the distance in Utah. The expanse held no resemblance at all to the New York City metropolitan area to which she was accustomed, with its buildings sprouting like stalagmites from the city's bowels.

A few minutes later, Lesley turned onto a dirt road, Indian Route 237, that disappeared into a canyon. At the canyon's edge the road actually ended for her and her Audi. She'd need Alan's Cherokee to make it any further, but she could see the place the receptionist had described to her just ahead.

The hogan rested right against the canyon wall, the back section appearing to melt into the wall itself. On the roof, solar panels sucked the sun's rays from the desert dry air. Cacti, mixed with mesquite and pinion trees, surrounded the exterior and rose as high as the roof in some places, providing protection from the wind and dust and a mine-field of obstacles to ward off possible intruders. A huge bay window covered the wall on the left side wall facing the canyon and away from the sun's path.

Lesley parked next to the Chevy truck in the driveway and sat for a minute listening though the open window to the invading silence. Only a hawk's cry in the distance pierced the quiet. She could feel the life around her, hidden from the daytime heat and dryness of the air. Nighttime there would bring a hive of activity with the desert cool climate.

Approaching the door to the hogan, she wondered what she'd say to David Nighteagle. Who was he anyway. Alan hadn't really offered much more to her than that she should talk with him and Shanee hadn't said much more. The receptionist did say that he made some fine flutes and told her the house would take a little while to get to and to make sure she had plenty of gas to get back to town.

She knocked on the hogan door. Waited. No response. Nothing moving around the place or any sounds from inside. She knocked again. Waited. Again, nothing. She walked around to the window and tried to peer into the sun-screened glass. Dark as a desert night. She went back to the front and tried the door handle. Unlocked. She opened it enough to shout in. She didn't want to walk in and get shot.

"Hello?" Nothing.

Louder.

"Hello?" Again, nothing.

The door opened easily. Now, the sound of flute music poured from the room. Eerie, haunting sounds with a steady rhythmic drum filling the timeless voids in the flute melody. She glanced around. Saw no one. Flutes of all shapes and sizes graced one wall of the room. An altar to the flute gods.

"David Nighteagle?" Still no response.

A curtained opening in the back of the room called to her. She delicately pulled back the canvas door.

"David Nighteagle?"

Artifacts lined shelves along one wall. Stores of canned foods, water containers, first aid supplies, gas cans filled the shelves on the other side of the room. Another canvas doorway led out of the back of the obvious storeroom. The closer she stepped to it, the louder she could hear another flute echoing from the doorway. This time the flute played solo. No drums. She pulled back the curtain.

A quite large cave opened up in front of her, lit by a blazing fire in the middle of the floor, smoke flowing upward into a funnel-shaped flue. On either side of the fire sat a man and woman, cross-legged, lotus-style, naked. The man's shoulder length black hair, held in place with a headband, showed streaks of silver. His body showed none of the degenerating signs of Western culture. No sagging skin or pot belly.

Across from him, the very pretty Native American woman reflected the same healthiness. Full, firm breasts. No tan lines. Soft, bronze skin that glowed in the firelight. Her glistening, long black hair hung in pig tails down her back, tied off with bows.

They both looked to be meditating. Lesley didn't want to disturb them, but she had come all this way and didn't want to leave without at least speaking to David Nighteagle, if that's who this was. She quietly called again.

"David Nighteagle." She walked a little closer.

"David--" The woman stirred, surprised Lesley.

"May I help you?" The woman remained motionless, eyes closed.

"My name is --"

"Lesley."

How did she know that? The woman now looked at Lesley.

"The center called and said you'd be out. I'm Marianna." Marianna unfolded her legs and stretched. She was even prettier this close. She massaged her legs, then grabbed a piece of cloth next to her and stood. She wrapped the cloth around her waist.

"You're here to see David. That's David." She pointed to the man. "But he won't be back for a while."

That didn't make sense to Lesley.

Marianna clarified. "His body is here. His spirit is elsewhere. I never know how long he might be gone. Maybe I can help you?"

"Alan Hall and another instructor from the Coyote Canyon Center mentioned that David had told my father,

Arthur Whitney, to contact a Hopi sorceress named, Pine Leaf. I wondered what it was concerning and if I could get the information to contact her myself."

"Pine Leaf is a very powerful Nagual, and, yes, a sorceress. Nagual has a more positive sound to it than sorcerer or sorceress."

"I'm sorry. I didn't know."

"Only David would be able to explain why he told your father to contact Pine Leaf. I can give you directions to her place though. She's very reclusive and usually only sees people if someone she knows tells her they're coming. And she doesn't normally see Bilaganna."

"She saw my father, I assume, so maybe she'll see me."

"I'll give you directions and something from David which will help you get to see her."

Marianna went into the store room. David remained peacefully silent. Where was he if he wasn't here? Was he just in a trance? Lesley wondered if this trance-like state that David was in related to an epileptic state, but without the convulsions. Did he believe he was somewhere else after he awakened? Or did he just convince himself he had gone somewhere else?

Marianna returned with a map and a flute. "Follow this map to Pine Leaf's hogan. When you get there, don't go directly to the door. Get out of your car and wait for her to come out. You can show her the flute and tell her why you're there at that time. She'll let you know if she'll see you. Or she'll tell you to get off her property."

"How will she know I'm there if I don't go to the door?"

"She'll know."

"Thank you for all of your help. I'd still like to talk with David some time."

"I'll get you a card on the way out. You can call him and set up a time to talk."

Marianna led Lesley through the store room into the front of the hogan. The place was so much bigger inside than it looked from the outside, especially with the cave in the back. They said their good-byes at the door, and Lesley went to her car and sat and studied the map. She'd be going back to Highway 160 and then east and north toward Cortez. She'd then take Indian Route 201 to an unnamed road, where Pine Leaf's hogan was located.

****

The hogan lay at the end of Sleeping Ute Mountain, underneath a peak known as The Knees. Unlike David Nighteagle's hogan, this one looked almost deserted. Very little sign of life. An old, rusted truck in back. No other vehicles. Some dilapidated structures. Was she at the right place? Lesley knew she had followed the instructions on the map. She'd park and wait to see if anyone came out.

The landscape for miles and miles gave Lesley a view of the real southwest. Occasional mesquite dotted the otherwise barren, sandy dirt floor. Tumble weed rolled and tumbled with the help of the unburdened wind. Rock formations and strings of scraggly mountains cropped up out of the terrain. And no one came to the door. Maybe Pine Leaf had gone somewhere. Marianna had said to stay at the car until invited in. She'd wait five more minutes.

Lesley checked her phone, only one bar, and noticed the front door to the hogan creep open and a short, stout woman in a Hawaiian muumuu appear in the doorway. She put the phone away and got out of the car and stood by the door. The woman watched for a moment and then waved for Lesley to come to her. As Lesley neared the hogan, the woman turned and entered, beckoning Lesley to follow.

Inside the hogan, Lesley immediately felt an overwhelming presence. Not necessarily from the woman but a more all-consuming vapor, like the steam from rain hitting the scorched pavement on a hot New York evening. The aroma of pinion , the same as in Mama Rosa's, filled the air. Dream catchers hung from the ceiling and by the windows. Blankets draped the walls and the furniture, what little furniture Lesley could see. A drum and some shakers occupied one area of the room. The woman adjusted a pot on a rock stove in the middle of the room, motioned for Lesley to sit on a bench next to the open flame. She poured water into two cups, handed one cup to Lesley and sat on the bench. Lesley could see tiny particles of leaf floating on the top of the water, took a whiff of the steeping tea. Sweet smelling, like Rose Hips.

"Drink. Then you can find your father." The woman pointed to the cup.

"Why would you think I'm looking for my father?" How could she know that?

"I know you. We met before."

"I've never seen you in my life." What was in this tea? "Are you Pine Leaf?"

"That name is how people know me." Pine Leaf sipped the tea. "You are the daughter of Ahote. My nephew sent you to me."

"If you mean David Nighteagle, a woman at his place sent me --"

"Flute girl. His woman. Lenmana. Nice girl." Pine Leaf motioned for Lesley to sip the tea.

Lesley barely wetted her lips with the drink. The bitter taste overpowered the sweetness of the tea's fragrance. "Who is this Ahote?"

"Ahote is your father. That name belongs to him now."

"Do you know where my father is?" Lesley hoped she'd skip all the other stuff and just tell her where Arthur went.

"When we last met he was preparing for a journey."

"Yes. To Lost Canyon." Maybe Pine Leaf knew where Arthur went in the canyon.

"His journey was into the second attention. He came to learn the seeing way."

"So he's not in the canyon."

"He's with the inorganic beings."

"Where is that exactly?"

"Only he and the inorganic beings know that."

"So he's lost then."

"Ahote is not lost."

"No one's seen him in almost a month." She thought for a moment.

Pine Leaf sipped the tea, motioned for Lesley to take a sip. She placed her lips on the rim of the cup and let the liquid trickle through. She felt a little light-headed.

"Can these inorganic beings help me find him?"

"You must enter the second attention to mingle with the inorganic beings."

"Let me get this right. My father, Ahote, is on a journey where only he knows where he is, but he's not lost."

Pine Leaf nods "yes".

"He's with some inorganic beings who no one can see unless they're where my father is."

Pine Leaf nods "yes" again.

"But he's still not lost."

Pine Leaf nods again.

"And you can't take me to him or show me where he is."

"I can only guide the seer to the path. The seer must take the journey alone. I showed Ahote magical passes to help guide him to find his path."

"Okay, this is getting a little ridiculous." She snapped. "I just want to find my father and get back to New York!" Lesley stopped and calmed herself. "I just want to know where my father is or what happened to him. How do I get to him?"

"You must look for him in the second attention."

"The second attention." Lesley decided to just go along with Pine Leaf. "Well how do I get to this second attention?"

"You can think of the every-day world as the first attention. That is the waking world we live in each day. The second attention is the realm in which our energy body exists, where all energy in the universe exists in its purest form."

"No body. Just energy."

"Yes. A complement to the physical body. It is open to many more possibilities than the physical body. It can recognize energy as a light or a vibration and feel pain or other sensations. It can use the flow of energy to travel unhindered throughout the universe."

"How do I get in touch with my energy body?"

"The journey to entering the second attention can be long and difficult. You must be dedicated and strong."

Leslie thought for a moment. This was getting weirder and weirder by the minute. Second attentions? Inorganic beings? Energy bodies? She hadn't bargained for all of the spiritualism. Should she continue with this or just get up and walk out?

"I want to find my father, whatever it takes."

Pine Leaf stares into Lesley's eyes, as if looking deep into her soul.

"First you must be cleansed. You must go to the sweat lodge. Go and see my nephew. He can help you."

"What is this sweat lodge thing?"

"The Bilaganna spirit differs from that of my people. Living in the Bilaganna world has tainted your spirit with wants and desires that weigh heavily upon you. The sweat lodge will cleanse your spirit. Then you can begin the seeing way."

"The only desire I have right now is to find my father or find out what has happened to him and get back to New York."

"Then you must find my nephew and enter the sweat lodge. He'll know what to do."

Lesley puts down the tea cup and gets up to leave. At the door she turns back.

"Just what does Ahote mean?"

"Restless one."

"That would be my father."

B. R. Fleming

7

tsosts'id

****

Sheriff Branshee's message reached Lesley just as she caught site of Cortez after leaving Pine Leaf's hogan.

"We've found a body in Lost Canyon. Can't tell much about it yet. They're taking it to the Coroner's office in Durango. It'll be at least a couple of days before we hear anything. I'll let you know."

Mixed emotions filled Lesley's thoughts. If the body was Arthur, she'd at least know what happened and could move on. The last of her family would be gone though. If it wasn't Arthur, she'd still have some hope that he had just gone off on his own and would return when he finished his work. She'd want to kick his ass for not letting anyone know, but she promised herself that she would mend the rift between them.

Meeting with Pine Leaf hadn't convinced Lesley that Arthur had done anything more than just wander off on one of his quirky expeditions. The notion that a person could leave his body and travel to another place, meet with some other-worldly beings, and then return as if nothing out of the ordinary had ever happened didn't fit with Lesley's way of thinking. Sure, she had dealt with people who entered other states of consciousness when experiencing seizures, but actually, spiritually, leaving one's body and travelling to another place or dimension or whatever they called it seemed quite ludicrous to her. Were Shamans and followers like David Nighteagle and Marianna just inducing a seizure-like state and imagining they were entering another realm of consciousness? She'd have to explore that idea a little further, depending on what happened with the body that Sheriff Branshee had found.

She dug out the card Marianna had given her with David Nighteagle's phone number and tried the number. No luck. His message gave her the address of his store in town and the times he would be there. She was getting the impression that time here was relative, that saying two o'clock actually meant more like two thirty or three or maybe not at all. She'd try David Nighteagle's store and then make a visit to the clinic that the CDC had told her to contact for instructions on the data collection.

The store was actually just a counter in a combination music and variety shop just off of Highway 160 in town, the variety being small appliances and electronics. The clerk really didn't expect David to be in that afternoon - "He doesn't usually come in unless he has an appointment to show a flute" - and didn't know when he might be coming next. Before Lesley left, she bought a new battery for her phone and got directions from the clerk to the clinic. She would stop by the inn and freshen up before venturing out again for the afternoon.

She had become comfortable in her room. Having the kitchenette helped and made the place feel almost like an apartment, like the hostels she had stayed in when travelling in Europe. Being on the second floor and at the end of the section kept the noise down, except for the traffic on the busy main highway. But that died down after the sun set. The light on her room phone caught her attention as she opened the door and threw her bag on the bed. She called the front desk.

"This is Dr. Whitney in room 223. Did you have a message for me?"

"Let me see." Silence. "We've got a package for you at the front desk. I can have someone bring it up to you if you like."

"Yes. That would be fine. Thank you."

"Yes, Ma'am."

This must be the package that Elliot had sent that had come from Arthur to her in New York. She'd forgotten all about it with everything else going on. She couldn't even imagine what it might be after all these years. It hadn't arrived around her birthday or any other important day that would make it a gift. Just another of Arthur's eccentric actions.

The Navajo boy that brought the package to her couldn't have been more than fifteen years old. Shouldn't he be in school? Just like in other parts of the country, the poor class or minority class or immigrant class held the service jobs. She'd noticed that the maids were all Native American women, girls, too, and that most of the people she'd seen at the manual labor type jobs were Native American. Well, it was the Southwest, and the native populations weren't really always the minority, but they did constitute the lower income class. She thought back to the rally and to the speech that she'd heard. Jobs, medical care, living assistance. No wonder the native populations felt so angry.

She took the package from the boy, tipped him well, and flopped on the bed. She'd expected it to be larger. It wasn't much bigger than a large box of matches. She ripped the perforated zip and emptied an exotic wooden box onto the bedspread. A Native American-style carving covered the top of the box. She'd seen the image somewhere before. In a dream? She gently opened the box, intrigued by what she might find inside.

Inside, the same image that appeared on the top of the box shone in a brilliant silver with turquoise inlay. The image featured a creature, not necessarily a man, but man-like. Two arms, two legs, standing erect but with its back curled and the right leg arched slightly. The creature looked to be playing a flute and had a humped back. The eyes of the creature glittered with ruby stones that caught the light and gave the face a haunting aura.   Lesley couldn't stop staring at the image. It mesmerized her. Who, rather, what was it?

She didn't want to disturb the piece but wanted to investigate it more closely and lifted it out of the box with her index finger and thumb. A finely woven, leather necklace, highlighted also with turquoise beads, attached to the pendant followed it out of the box. She'd never seen anything like it before. Fragile. Exquisite. Stuffed into the packaging she saw a folded piece of paper. She pulled the paper out of the box and unfolded it. She recognized the scribble on the message immediately. Years of writing hurriedly on blackboards and in notebooks had caused Arthur's handwriting to deteriorate to an almost indistinguishable hieroglyphic that only the closest people to him could decipher.

Take good care of this.

Subtle. Straightforward. Composed by a master of brevity. This wasn't just a gift. Lesley realized the implications. Arthur would never have sent the necklace to her if it didn't hold huge importance to him and if he didn't feel that he could keep it safe. But safe from what? Judging from the fine craftsmanship and detail and the gems that ornamented it, the value could be astronomical both in monetary and historical terms.

She thought about putting it back in the box, hiding it, but decided that it would be safest with her. She pulled some of the packaging out of the box, wrapped the note around the necklace and then placed it in the packaging and in a pocket of her messenger bag. She always had that bag with her and would be able to follow Arthur's wish. Now she needed to go by the clinic and introduce herself to the staff there and then see if she could find David Nighteagle. She'd take a run out to the center and see if Alan could help her find him. A good excuse to see Alan again. A thought of Jonathan crossed her mind that she dismissed as quickly as it had appeared.

✶✶✶✶✶✶✶✶✶✶✶✶✶✶✶✶✶✶✶✶✶✶✶✶✶✶✶✶✶

Lesley's visit to the clinic hadn't gone exactly as she had anticipated. Instead of welcoming her help with collecting data for use by the CDC to trigger further resources for the area, the Charge Nurse and what appeared to be the only doctor on duty grilled Lesley about her qualifications and about who had sent her there and why the clinic needed her to do their work. Lesley tried to explain to them that she was merely there to help and tried to assure them that she wouldn't interfere with their duties, but the idea of someone coming from the federal government for any reason put everyone on the defensive. Everyone in the region seemed to feel that way. Lesley left her card and the number of the assistant director from the CDC with the Charge Nurse so that she could verify the reason for Lesley's visit.

Walking back to her car, she noticed a man leaning against the front of a Chevy pickup parked next to her car, following her with his eyes. She didn't think anything of it at first, but then a flash of recognition blazed through her mind. She'd seen him somewhere before. But where? She wrestled with the thought of going back into the clinic and waiting for him to leave but reached into her bag and pulled out the key, ready to punch the panic button if need be. She was almost to the car anyway and could probably make it inside before he could get around to her. She unlocked the door and started to open it.

"They don't trust you, you know. Most people around here won't." Now she remembered who he was.

Lesley paused, opened the door slightly, ready to jump in. "Because I'm not from around here."

"Partly. But they see plenty of people from the outside world. You represent something even more threatening."

"And what would that be?" This was the man from the rally who spoke to the people. Bold Sun?

"Bilaganna society. The government. The destroyers of our culture."

"I'm a doctor. I'm sworn to heal. I help people."

"To them you're just another official intruder, Dr. Whitney."

Now he really had her attention. "How do you know my name?"

"I know that you're a professor at Columbia University. You specialize in epidemiology. You're here to find out what happened to your father, Arthur Whitney."

Lesley could feel the wave of astonishment spreading over her face.

"We're not all ignorant savages, Dr. Whitney."

"What is it you want?" Lesley's grip on the key tightened, ready to punch the panic button. Or what?

"Your father got into something he should have left alone. You should pack up and go back to Columbia, back to your Bilaganna life. You won't find what you're searching for here."

"And what if I don't want to go yet?"

"You may not like what you find." Bold Sun got into the pickup, poked his head through the window. "You don't belong here." He drove off, leaving Lesley staring after.

Lesley stood by the open car door, unable to move. This was all more than she had bargained for. What had Arthur gotten himself into this time? She just wanted to get back to her research and classes and get this all over with. But she'd never be able to work again, to concentrate on her work, if she left now.

She slipped into the driver's seat and started the engine. Bold Sun's warning ran through her mind. What had he meant that Arthur had gotten into something he shouldn't have? Should she try to find David Nighteagle? Or, should she just go back to the inn and pack her bags? No, she wouldn't be scared away! She'd come to find out what happened to Arthur and wouldn't leave until she did, whatever way that turned out.

****

The center looked deserted when she pulled up in front of the lodge. She walked up onto the lodge porch and saw a group of students in the dining area sculpting mugs and animal figures. The rocking chairs invited her to relax and enjoy the peacefulness of the afternoon. She couldn't stop now though, as much as she would love to do so. She'd have never even thought about it back at Columbia.

Lesley strode along the walkway to the research building. No one at the reception desk. Gift shop closed until four o'clock. Probably opens when the students finish their classes. Even the offices that encircled the stairwell gave the impression that they'd been vacant for years. She could hear activity in the basement, a low hum of student voices and an occasional thud that sounded like heavy bags being stacked on one another. Maybe she'd check down there.

"Hello, may I help you?" A man dressed half business and half casual poked his head out from one of the seemingly vacant offices, startling Lesley.

"Oh. Well, yes, maybe you can. I'm looking for Alan Hall."

"Alan's up at the Pueblo Learning Center with a class. Can I help you with something. I'm Barry, Barry Randall. I'm the center director."

"I'm Lesley, Whitney. I just needed to talk with Alan for a minute."

"Oh, my goodness. Lesley Whitney, Arthur's daughter. Alan mentioned that you were here. I was hoping I'd get to meet you. Can I first tell you how sorry we all are about Arthur's disappearance. It's just shocking."

"Yes, it's been a bit of a shock to me too. When do you think Alan will be done?"

"Let's see." He checks his smart phone. "They finish up there about four, so another couple of hours."

"I really just needed to ask him something, and I couldn't get him on his phone."

"Instructors can't accept personal calls during their classes. It's only about five minutes up the hill. I can take you to him and watch his class while you talk."

"Okay. Thank you." Lesley followed Barry out of the building and onto the field in front of the lodge.

"It's up on the side of that ridge." Barry pointed to an incline in front of them. A dirt road cut through the juniper and mesquite trees that blanketed the side of the hill. Lesley could see the structure now at the top of the ridge, an L-shaped building with a tower attached which resembled an old Spanish mission. She wished she had some hiking boots and had worn them instead of the flats. She'd find some boots in town, leave them in the car from now on, and bring a change of clothes with her. She gradually was learning how to function in this quite different terrain and climate.

"This new learning center has doubled the activities we can offer students. It provides an authentic habitat in which the students can recreate the same everyday activities the Pueblo people performed."

Barry sounded like a director, promoting his cause to investors. "What exactly was dad's connection to the center?"

"Arthur didn't really have anything to do with the educational aspect of the center but more the research function. He'd discovered several of the sites that we eventually surveyed and excavated. Part of his funding came from the grants that we received to excavate those sites."

"What took him into Lost Canyon? Alan said that the canyon was too remote and rugged for students and that the center had no interest in it."

"Arthur had found some old Spanish documents that spoke of a great Kiva in this area that had special significance with the early Puebloan people who settled here. He set his life's work to finding that Kiva."

"A great Kiva?" Lesley's breathing had gotten more difficult with the climb up to the ridge.

"All Pueblo settlements, from the earliest mud and thatch pit houses to the later cliff houses in the canyons, contained a special room, a Kiva, where the elders and Shamen of the tribes would gather for sacred ceremonies. The early Kivas were circular structures dug a few feet into the ground and covered with a mud and thatch roof, like a dome home. In the later cliff houses, the Kivas were dug out of the cliff ledge with a single opening in the top and a ladder to enter and exit. They remained circular, usually about twenty feet in diameter by about eight feet high. The Puebloan people were fairly short in stature. A great Kiva usually would measure anywhere from thirty to fifty feet in diameter and would be a regional meeting place for the elders of several tribes."

"Is that what makes it special?"

"That's what intrigued Arthur about this particular one. Just being a great Kiva wasn't anything special. This region contains a number of great Kivas. Chaco Canyon. Canyon de Chelly. Aztec Ruins."

"But, I still don't understand the fascination with Lost Canyon."

"It's about the only place around here that hasn't been thoroughly explored for sites. Prospectors, railroad engineers, miners have been going in and out of there for years and never have reported any sites or remarkable remains. But it's huge too. It's stretches from Dolores east for about a hundred miles with lots of side canyons and outlets."

They had now reached the ridge and the structure. Students ground corn and thrashed wheat, played drums and danced, molded mud bricks and stomped around in a mud hole, splashing water on one another. One group off to the side of the building used spears and a wooden stick to simulate hunting a turkey. Another used some of the mud and branches and twigs to repair a hole in a small, dome-shaped hut. The whole area was alive with activity. And right in the middle of it all Alan worked with the group of students repairing the hole in the mud hut.

"There's Alan. I'll go get him and tell him you'd like to talk with him." Barry took his time, talking with the different groups of students and the instructors on his way over to Alan.

Lesley waited and watched the students. Could she do this? Work with this age group? They looked like middle-schoolers. Twelve? Thirteen? So much energy. They made her tired just watching them. She had been teaching college her entire life, had never even gotten a teaching degree, but had been around Arthur during his classes and with Elliot enough to learn from them. She'd definitely have to take some education courses to be able to work with anyone younger than college-age students.

Alan finally made his way over to her. He hadn't shaven in probably a few days. Mud covered his clothes, his arms, and even nested in his hair. He looked irresistibly cuter for it. He had a few inches height on Jonathan and had a more muscular build. Lesley hadn't really allowed herself to even notice anyone except Jonathan for years, and Alan was awakening some feelings that she had buried for all that time.

"Hey. What are you doing out this way?"

"I need to find David Nighteagle. I've tried his phone and shop in town but can't get him."

"What do you need with David?" Alan brushed the mud from his arms and hair. Cleaning up for her?

"His aunt, Pine Leaf, sent me to find him. She said I needed to go to the sweat lodge and be cleansed."

A grin spread across Alan's face. "You're sure she said a sweat lodge. That's heavy duty spiritualism for an east coast city girl."

Was he making fun of her? "Yes. I'm sure. What are you smiling about?"

"It's nice to see you."

Lesley felt her face flush. "So, do you know how I can get in touch with David?"

"He's a pretty busy guy with his performances and flute business."

Now she was getting frustrated. "Shit. I'll find him myself." She turns and walks away.

Alan stops her. Turns her to him. "Wait. I'm sorry."

Lesley calms down. "Look, some things have come up that I need to check on, and I don't have a whole lot of time to do all this.

"Let me make a few calls. I think I can find him. Are you busy tonight?"

Was he asking her on a date? "Not necessarily. Why?"

"You said you needed a sweat lodge. I've got to get back to the students. Call me about five." He turned and headed back to the students. Stopped. Turned back. "And dress comfortably." He grinned.

✳✳✳✳✳✳✳✳✳✳✳✳✳✳✳✳✳✳✳✳✳✳✳✳✳✳✳✳

Lesley hadn't taken this long to get ready to go out in years. Alan had told her to meet him at David's place just after dark, which she figured meant about eight o'clock. She hadn't brought anything really comfortable with her, so she stopped at a shop on her way back to the inn and bought some jeans, loose, not the skinny kind, and a Navajo design flannel shirt. New hiking boots and the necklace from Arthur completed her "comfortable" look. As long as she had the necklace with her, she knew it would be safe, and she didn't have that much jewelry anyway. Maybe Alan or David could tell her something about the image on the necklace.

She pulled into David Nighteagle's place with the sun casting its last rays over the horizon. She could barely make out a Chevy truck and Alan's Cherokee parked in front of the hogan and pulled the Audi in next to the Cherokee. Maybe she should go back to the rental place and see about getting an SUV or something a little more suited to the dirt roads and rugged terrain instead of the Audi. She got out and stood by the car, waiting, as she had been told, for someone to come out and invite her in. Would they be able to see her out there?

The hogan door opened and Alan, followed by David and Marianna, stepped out onto the dirt and walked to Lesley.

"Nice shirt. Going for a hike?"

"You said dress comfortably. This is it."

"It's great. Come on. We're going to ride with David and Marianna."

They all piled into the front of David's Chevy truck. A tight squeeze, but they managed. The nearly full moon had just begun to peek out from behind Mesa Verde to the east and lit the entire landscape with a blue tint, outlining the rock formations, mesquite and pinion trees that lined the highway. Lesley appreciated the tight fit in the front seat now that the sun had gone down and the night air held a brisk chill. Alan's arm around her neck on the top of the seat helped. Cozy. Each day that she spent here made her realize more and more Arthur's attraction to the Southwest.

"I'm sorry we didn't get to speak the other day." David's voice had a peaceful, musical quality, a reassuring tone of tranquility.

"I didn't want to disturb your meditation."

"The second attention differs from meditation. In the second attention you lose consciousness of your present reality. Marianna told me you'd come by. I had no idea you'd been there."

"Pine Leaf mentioned something to me about the second attention. She told me something very strange. She was talking pretty crazy." Lesley waited for a response. None came.

"She said my father wasn't lost, that he was on a journey. And, that I could see him if I entered the second attention." Lesley again expects a reaction. Gets none.

"Well, isn't that an odd thing to say to someone whose father has disappeared in a lost canyon and who may be the dead body that the sheriff found there?"

Marianna finally responded. "Pine Leaf is a Nagual. She knows the seeing way and magical passes to help one enter the second attention. She can enter the second attention and leave it at will. She knows the ways of the inorganic beings."

"She mentioned them too. She said my father was on a journey with them, not lost."

David stopped the truck next to a beehive-shaped mound and turned off the engine. "If anyone would know, Pine Leaf would. We're here."

Everyone piled out of the truck. David and Marianna walked to the mound and squatted next to an old Native American man by a fire. Alan started to walk away, but Lesley grabbed his arm and stopped him.

"Do you believe what Pine Leaf said?"

"I've seen and heard about some pretty strange events since I've been here. I know that these people believe it. I haven't made up my mind about it yet."

"But this second attention and inorganic beings. It sounds like Area 54 and alien visitations or something."

Alan thinks better of correcting Lesley. "Lots of people believe in that stuff too. Come on."

Alan leads Lesley to the mound. Lesley stops him again.

"We're all going to get into that little thing?" The lodge looked more like a big mud oven than anything else.

"Easily."

Stopping outside, everyone, except Lesley, begins taking off clothes. The old man strips naked and enters the mound. David and Marianna strip naked. Alan begins to remove his shirt. Lesley renews her grip on Alan's arm.

"You know, I wasn't really prepared for this." Lesley now understood the grin on Alan's face from earlier in the day.

"It's okay. You do whatever is comfortable for you. The purpose is to cleanse the physical body as well as the soul. Your clothes will be soaking wet in a few minutes from the steam if you leave them on. And you won't get the full effect of the sweat lodge either."

Alan strips down to nothing. Lesley, not to be outdone, slowly strips, hesitating before peeling off her bra and panties. She follows Alan to the mound, trying to not be too obvious in her attempts to cover herself. They wait in front, in the moonlight. Lesley could feel Alan's eyes roaming over her, or at least she thought so. But she had her own surveying going on.

Alan breaks the silence, whispering to Lesley. "In a minute, Running Foot will call us in. He'll be the only one to speak. He'll sing four chants. Then we'll come out, refresh, and go back in for another four chants."

"What if I feel faint or get claustrophobic or something?"

"Leaving during the sing breaks the whole unity of energy. It disrupts the spiritual connection."

"Just tough it out then, right?"

"If you feel faint, just lay back. I'll help you out when the chants are over. You don't have to go back for the second bath."

Laying back didn't sound like a great thing to do in there. "I think I'll be okay."

"At some point, Running Foot will ask if anyone wants to give thanks to the spirits. That's your chance to say something to your ancestors, to Arthur, to the earth mother, or to whomever you wish. You don't have to though."

David turns to Lesley. "This is about as close as you will get to entering the second attention without actually entering dream state."

"This is one of the magical passes?"

"Yes, it is. A minor one."

Running Foot calls from inside. They crowd into the darkened lodge, sitting on blankets placed around a stack of hot stones in a pit centered in the lodge floor. A dull glow of coals around and under the stack of rocks provides the only light in the lodge. Smoke, dry heat engulf the room. Bodies glisten with sweat. Slowly, Lesley's eyes acclimate to the darkness. Running Foot sings the first chant, indicates to David to wet the stones. Steam fills the lodge. The steam heat enters Lesley's lungs, burns her eyes. Tears pour down her cheeks, mix with the sweat beads popping out on her face, spill onto her breasts. Her nipples burn. How long can she stay?

The second chant is sung. David saturates the rocks a second time, steam bursting into the air, billowing to the top of the lodge and flowing through the tiny space. Lesley's whole body tingles. Sweat drips from every pore of her body. She barely makes out the shapes of the others through the dense fog. Running Foot sings the final chants. One by one they each exit the lodge. They all fall to the ground, drained from the heat. David and Marianna roll in the sandy soil. Alan and Lesley sprawl against a rock, Lesley still a little self-conscious.

"What are they doing?"

"They're removing the dead skin."

"How do they even have the energy to move."

A few minutes later, Running Foot calls for them to reenter the lodge. Running Foot sings the first chants. He then indicates time to give thanks.

David begins. "We the five-fingered beings are related to the four-legged, the winged beings, the spiritual beings, Father Sky, Mother Earth. We are all relatives. We cannot leave our relatives behind."

Running Foot chants.

Marianna goes next. "Changing Woman of many faces, we bless and thank you for all you give us. All fortune that is mine is because of you."

Again, Running Foot chants.

Alan follows. "Thank you grandfather for all you give us. Thank you grandmother for your blessings and for the abundance of your offering."

Lesley remains silent, can only think of the steam and heat and the difficulty in breathing. Running Foot, indicates to David to douse the stones. Steam chokes the air in the lodge. Lesley reacts to the steam heat, dizzily falling forward toward the stones, but being stopped before falling into them, pulled back upright, held still. She opens her eyes. Hidden in the steam mist she sees a figure. Strong hands grip her shoulders, steadying her. She looks into two steel blue eyes.

"Dad?" She closes her eyes, tries to shake the dizziness.

Running Foot sings the final chant, picks up a bowl, sips, passes the bowl. The others sip from the bowl. Alan passes the bowl to Lesley. She shakily holds the bowl to her lips and sips, spilling the liquid over her. Running Foot takes the bowl, pours the remainder of liquid on the stones. They all sit quietly for a moment. Lesley rests her head on Alan's shoulder, leans into him feeling the warmth of his skin against her. David gets up, leads everyone out.

Alan helps Lesley out. Lesley stumbles to the ground, rests against a rock, while David and Marianna frolic in the dirt. Alan places a blanket on Lesley. David and Marianna begin getting dressed.

"Are you okay?"

"I got very light-headed." She catches her breath. "For a moment. I began falling. Someone grabbed me and held me. That must have been you. I know it sounds absurd, but I thought I saw my Dad."

"I didn't catch you."

She looks to David and Marianna. Not them either?

Lesley puts her head down. "What is going on here?"

David squats next to Lesley. "Pine Leaf has started you on the seeing way. If your father is with the inorganic beings, she will help you find him."

"This is all just too much. First the tornado at Dad's hogan, then the dead body in Lost Canyon, this weird necklace Dad sent me, and now this."

Alan sat and put on his boots. "What tornado?"

"When I went to the hogan with the Sheriff, this strange wind blew through while we were there. It kind of knocked me down. I heard drums, and I thought I saw a figure dancing. Then it felt like people grabbing at me, holding me down."

Marianna sits with them. "That sounds like the Airs playing tricks with you."

"The Airs?" Marianna helps Lesley get dressed.

"They're spirits, like poltergeists. They use wind to annoy you. They're not usually dangerous. Just mischievous."

Alan cuts in. "Arthur sent you a necklace?"

Lesley digs into her shirt pocket and pulls out the necklace. A flash of recognition shakes her. "Now I remember where I saw this image. That's the figure that I saw in the cloud of dust in the hogan."

"May I see that?" Lesley hands the necklace to David.

"Did your father say where he got this?"

"No. He sent it to me at the university. They sent it to me out here. He wrapped it and put it in a box with a note that said, 'take good care of this'."

"Kokopelli. That's the image. Another mischief-maker. He plays his flute and brings fertility to the people and the land."

Alan moves closer to look at the necklace. "Better keep the young maidens locked up when Kokopelli comes to the village. Why would Arthur send this to you instead of just keeping it himself?"

David gives the necklace back to Lesley. "Go back to Pine Leaf. Show her the necklace. She'll know about it."

Lesley places the necklace in her shirt pocket. Finishes dressing. David talks with Running Foot. Hands him a bag. Alan and Lesley go to the truck and get in the front seat.

Lesley lays her head back on Alan's arm. "I need to go to Lost Canyon. Can you take me there?"

"What do you think you'll find that the Sheriff and his men didn't find?"

"I don't know. Probably nothing. But if Dad went there, I want to at least know that I went there and followed up on him."

"When do you want to go?" Alan smiled.

"I need to go back to Pine Leaf tomorrow evening. Can we go around noon tomorrow?"

"I'll get Shanee to take the class in the afternoon."

"Thank you. And I'll be wearing my hiking boots." She smiled and looked up into his eyes. Their eyes locked.

David and Marianna climb in the front seat beside Lesley. David starts the engine. Lesley settles into Alan's side, lets her head rest on the back of the seat. The moon had risen high in the sky and shone bright enough that David could drive the highway without using his headlights. Lesley closed her eyes and relished the rhythm of the truck following the contours of the highway. She could never do this in New York. Slowly, she succumbed to the day's drain on her energy and drifted off into a half sleep of sorts, that midway point of peacefulness between consciousness and dreamland. If tomorrow turned out to be anything like today, she would need all the rest she could get.

The Secret People

8

tseebíí

****

Lesley awoke to her phone playing one of her favorite songs from Hall and Oates, *One on One*. That meant Jonathan. Should she answer it? She dug the phone out of her bag. Coffee would be nice about now.

"Hi." She moved to the kitchenette to start the coffee.

"Hey! When are you coming back? I miss you so much."

"I miss you too." Did she? "I don't know yet. Haven't heard anything yet about the body they found. I'm kind of waiting to hear about that before I make any plans." Water in. Coffee packet in. Start.

"I'm not gonna be able to get away. Too much going on with the class. I really hoped you'd be back sooner."

"I've been gone less than a week."

"Well, each day feels like a week." She couldn't decide if that was sweet or pathetic.

"I can't leave here until I know what's happened to Dad, no matter how long that takes. You can understand that, can't you?"

"Les, . . . I'm sorry. I'm being selfish. Of course I understand."

"I need to get going."

"Busy day?"

"I'm going to visit one of the sites Dad had been working."

"You be careful out there. You shouldn't be going to those places by yourself."

"I'm not. One of the archaeologists from the center is taking me out there."

"Oh?"

"He did some work with Dad, and he knows the area." She wouldn't tell him about the sweat lodge just yet. Maybe when she got back. "I really do need to get going though."

"Okay. But you call me later when you get back. And make sure your phone battery is charged."

"Of course I will."

They said their goodbyes, and Lesley took her coffee and a muffin she'd bought at the health food store and camped out in the bathroom to get ready for the day. This wouldn't be a day for dressing comfy. She'd be prepared this time. Hiking boots, plenty of water, the new Swiss Army knife and hat she picked up at the mercantile store. The new backpack would carry extra water, batteries, a camera, spare cell phone battery, trail mix and Tiger's Milk protein bars, another shirt, and some necessities the clerk told her she might need. Yes, she would definitely be prepared this time.

✳✳✳✳✳✳✳✳✳✳✳✳✳✳✳✳✳✳✳✳✳✳✳✳✳✳✳✳

Alan had called and asked if they could leave a little early, so Lesley had had to rush some to get ready. He drove a different vehicle this time, an older model Land Rover S1 that he said would be better suited than his

Cherokee for the rougher terrain of the canyon. The Land Rover found every slight variation of the pavement, even on the seemingly level highway leading to the canyon. Lesley couldn't even imagine what the ride would be like when they got there. With the top and doors off and the oversize tires, the noise allowed for little or no real conversation, only the occasional short burst of comment.

"How long did you work with dad?"

"Pretty much since he arrived a couple of years ago. We started the Yellow Jacket dig. I'm still working that one.

"And Dad?"

"Well, you know your dad."

"We lost touch the past few years."

"He's really not much on the digging part. He likes to do the searching, the exploring, and then investigate the findings."

"I never knew that about him." She actually couldn't recall ever seeing Arthur dig at a site.

"It was only sheer luck that I found that map in with Arthur's stuff at the center."

"He always did prefer the less technical ways of doing things."

"I don't think I've ever even seen him on a computer."

"I'm surprised he even has a mobile phone." They both grinned at this. Lesley liked Alan's smile.

They veered off of the main highway onto a dirt road. Though dusty, the noise level dropped considerably.

"Most of the great Kivas in the southwest were excavated in the early 1900's and with crude technologies. None have even been found since. If this is a Kiva that's marked on Arthur's map, this could be a major archaeological discovery."

"I thought the center wasn't interested in excavating in Lost Canyon."

"A find like this could attract a lot of money to the center. We wouldn't bring the students up here to work. We'd excavate it ourselves and just bring the students to observe and study the site."

The road narrowed to one lane with a cliff wall on the driver side and a several hundred foot incline on the other. Lesley peered over the steep drop of the cliff and held on tight to the handle on the dash, balancing her coffee in the other hand, moving like a contortionist in anticipating the dips and bumps of the cliff-hugging road.

"Pretty rough through here. Should smooth out soon though." Alan didn't look bothered one bit by any of the perils in their path.

"I can't wait." She tightened her grip on the handle.

After a couple of miles, the road meandered into a canyon and smoothed out noticeably. Lesley relaxed and sipped her coffee. Only lukewarm now. But she still finished it. The canyon walls on both sides rose up for at least a hundred feet. Ahead, the cliff walls narrowed so that the Land Rover could go no further. Alan stopped and shut off the engine.

"Looks like we hike from here. If we've followed the map right, whatever it is Arthur marked on here should be about a quarter of a mile through this pass."

They grab backpacks, water bottles. Lesley wraps a bandana around her neck, puts on the new hat. Alan pulls a Colt pistol out of the glove box.

"What's that for?"

"Snakes, mainly. But you never know." Alan snatches a walking stick from the back of the Land Rover.

"Here. This might come in handy too."

"Don't you want to use it?"

"I'll pick one up along the way."

Alan takes the lead and heads into the narrow pass. Lesley follows close behind. They walk quietly and quickly through the rubble and boulders strewn in the narrow passageway. As they move further into the pass, the air becomes stiller and warmer. Lesley uses her free hand to undo the bandanna and wipe the sweat off her face, keeps one eye on Alan in front of her and one on the cliffs, watching for falling rock and rattlesnakes. The walking stick helped. Another item she'd need to pick up in town. Alan stops.

"Wait here a second." He climbs across a rock and into a thicket of Mesquite bushes, comes back with a dead-looking branch, pulls a knife from a holder on his belt, trims off the dead twigs and fashions a handle. Tests the stick. Lesley takes a slug of her water. Alan does the same.

"Okay. Ready?" He moves on without waiting for her response. She follows.

Lesley feels a cool breeze wash across her face, and the pass opens up onto an outcrop overlooking another canyon. Alan stops and pulls the map out of his bag, studies it. Looks out over the canyon. The canyon stretches for miles and out of sight to the right and the left with a several hundred foot drop to the bottom. A hundred yards across from the outcrop, the canyon wall mirrors the steep cliff below Lesley's feet, jagged rocks and patches of shale dotting the embankment.

"We're at the right spot." He takes binoculars out of his bag and surveys the canyon again. "I don't see anything unusual, nothing that would suggest a cliff house or pueblo."

He scans again. Stops. "Looks like a path over to the right. I'll go check it out. Why don't you wait here."

Lesley drops her backpack and sits on a rock in the shade. She watches as Alan scales the incline to the right and disappears across a boulder blocking the way along the ledge. A hawk floats into the canyon from above. Lesley follows the hawk's route as it rides the airwaves, coursing through the chasm. Her mind wanders. The hawk's cry pierces the air, reverberates on the canyon walls. She drifts into the memory of falling and suddenly awakening on a ledge, Arthur stares down at her, calling her name ever so gently. "Les. Les. Don't move. I've got to check on Conrad." Again the hawk calls to her.

A whistle shakes Lesley from the daydream. She gathers her wits and looks around and sees Alan standing on the boulder waving for her to come. She grabs the backpack and begins the climb to the boulder, Alan disappearing once more. She climbs the boulder and sees a box canyon about fifty feet further to the right with a narrower than narrow ledge leading to it. Alan stands at the opening waving for Lesley to follow.

Lesley hugs the cliff as she makes her way along the ledge to the opening. If she had let herself, she would have been too frightened to go on, but she wasn't going to let Alan know just how scared she really was. She tried not to look down at the canyon floor, keeping her focus about ten feet in front of her. That helped.

She reaches the opening and enters the inlet and sees Alan peering at her through a window of a cliff house tower. His grin convinces Lesley that he's quite pleased with himself. The structure was not very large, not anything like the Mesa Verde houses and was nestled into the cliff wall just enough for its presence to go undetected by anyone on the mesa above or by travellers in the main canyon below. Alan had disappeared and reappeared on the ground level from behind the tower, investigating every window and doorway.

He stopped at an opening in the ground in a small courtyard next to a waist-high wall. "This has to be what Arthur was searching for." He motioned for Lesley to come, took a flashlight from his backpack and knelt down, stuck his head into the hole and studied the interior with the flashlight.

"Amazing!" His voice sounded weird echoing from inside the chamber. "You've got to see this!"

"What? I can't hear you very well."

He sat up. "You've got to see it. It's huge. The room extends well into the cliff, much further than the wall up here."

"So, this is the Kiva? How do we get into it?"

"I really don't think you'll find Arthur in there. I don't see any signs of entry or anyone being in the area recently. I think we'd find something up here or see some gear if anything had happened to him here. No animal tracks or bird droppings that I can see."

Lesley gives him an "I need to know" look.

Alan sits up, opens his backpack and pulls out a rope. "We climb." He pulls a small bag out of the backpack, tosses the bag to the side.

"What can I do to help?"

He hands Lesley the bag. "Grab the hammer and a couple of the spikes. Start hammering one into the ground right behind me here. Get it far enough in to that mark level with the ground."

Lesley takes one of the spikes, notices a painted line about two inches from the top, and hammers the spike into the solid ground, checking every few seconds that the spike doesn't move around. Alan grins as Lesley struggles with the hammer. Lesley ignores him and continues banging away on the spike, determined to get it all the way into the ground. She gets it in.

"Now hammer the other one in about a foot in front of that one."

Lesley gets the second spike into the dirt, and Alan ties the end of the rope to the first stake and then wraps the rope around the second stake and ties it off. He drops the remainder of the rope into the opening.

"I don't imagine you've done much rope climbing, but it's really not that far down. I'll go down first. Drop my backpack to me when I get down there. Use the knots on the rope to keep yourself from slipping. "

Lesley reaches into her backpack, and pulls out leather gloves. "These should help." She smiles. Alan smiles back.

Alan climbs down. His voice echoes from inside the chamber. "All right. Drop the backpack to me."

Lesley lets the backpack drop into Alan's hands. "Go ahead and drop yours down now." She drops hers down next and starts the climb down. Not as easy as she thought, especially climbing backwards down the hole.

"Use the knots."

"I am using them."

Lesley clears the opening and hesitates in the darkness.

"I can't see anything."

"Let me help. Come down a little further."

Lesley slides down another notch, and Alan wraps his arms around her legs.

"Sit on my shoulder."

Lesley sits, still holding onto the rope, and Alan helps her step onto the floor of the Kiva.

"Thanks." She tries to get her bearings, but the darkness makes her feel dizzy. "It's hard to see anything."

Alan switches his flashlight to the "lantern" setting and hangs it from the rope. The room now becomes much more visible, at least for the surrounding twenty or so feet.

"Much bigger than I expected."

"You won't see many like this one.

Lesley takes her flashlight out of her backpack and scans the chamber. Alan wanders off to explore, snatching an extra flashlight from his backpack. A painting on one wall captures Lesley's attention. The wall art depicts a surreal scene with a man lying on a funeral bier and a hawk suspended above, the two connected by sunlight-type beams projecting upward from the man's body to the hawk. Striations - or were those cracks in the wall? - stemming from the hawk's wings and tail gave the impression of the hawk circling above the body.

Lesley stood for several moments studying the representation, hoping that if she stared at it long enough, it might reveal some hidden secret of the Kiva or some indication of her father's location to her. Nothing happened. Alan appeared from out of the darkness.

"Not much going on in here. But I need more light to really get a look at the place. Find anything interesting?"

"Just this painting."

Alan takes a closer look. "It appears pretty old, but sometimes people come in and paint on the walls in the ruins to try to fool the Bilaganna. We'll have to test the paint to determine the real age of it, and I don't have the materials I need with me to do that. Anyway, we better get going if we're going to get you back for your meeting."

Lesley starts back toward the rope and stumbles, drops her flashlight. Alan helps her up. They stand face to face, the dim lighting barely outlining their figures. Lesley stares into Alan's eyes.

"Thank you."

Alan pulls Lesley to him, kisses her. She freezes, not really prepared for his move, not really wanting to stop him. He wraps his arms tightly around her. She doesn't resist. The kiss lingers, their tongues exploring. His leg slips in between her legs, hands begin to roam over her back. She settles onto his leg, wraps one leg around his. He moves a hand to caress her breast, unbuttons the top buttons of her shirt and moves his hand inside. Her nipple responds to his touch, a flood of sensation coursing through her body. Alan begins kissing Lesley's neck, moves her shirt off of her shoulder, kisses his way down to Lesley's breast, circles the nipple with his tongue. She wraps her arms around his head, pulling him to her and pushing him away simultaneously. His hand slides down her back and into her pants, slipping into her panties. A cry of a hawk pierces the silence of the chamber, brings Lesley back to the Kiva. She gently pushes him aside, pulls away. They both collapse onto the Kiva wall, catching their breath.

"We should be getting going." She pulls her shirt on, straightens her clothing.

Alan breathes heavily. "Yes, I guess we should."

They gather their backpacks and climb back up the rope. Outside, Lesley breaks the awkward silence.

"Shouldn't we tell the Sheriff about the Kiva, so he can check out the area?" Alan knew what Lesley was thinking.

He takes Lesley's hand. "We can't tell anyone about this yet, not even the Sheriff. I'm sure if Arthur had wanted anyone else to know about it, he would have told them. Let's get back to town. I'll get some gear together, and we'll plan to come back and do a thorough search of the place."

Lesley nods agreement.

They trekked back to the Land Rover and drove back to Cortez. Alan dropped Lesley off at the Inn and told her to call him when she got back from her visit with Pine Leaf later that evening. She felt a pang of excitement remembering the Kiva, anticipating what may come later. She was being pulled in so many directions that she didn't know what to think now, and the more she learned, the more she experienced, the more confusing the whole situation became. Her only escape from the confusion rested in the belief that whatever did happen to Arthur had most likely been what Arthur had wanted. Any other explanation just didn't make sense.

B. R. Fleming

9

náhást'éí

****

The glow from the fire pit bathed Pine Leaf as she inspected the Kokopelli necklace, examining every bead and gem, sparks rising from the fire creating a meteor-shower spectacle against the darkened ceiling and funneling through the central vent opening. Lesley fidgeted, still uncomfortable sitting without a chair. She sipped the tea Pine Leaf had given her. It didn't taste as bitter as before.

Pine Leaf placed the necklace on a stone tablet in front of her. "Ahote searched for a place, a Kiva known only to the old ones who settled here in the beginning of time."

"He found it, we think."

"When the old ones came they had no knowledge of the seeing way." Pine Leaf pointed to the necklace. "Kokopelli brought the seeing way to the human beings. He taught the old ones so they could pass the knowledge on to those who followed."

"Is the Kiva that my fa-, that Ahote found where Kokopelli showed the old ones the seeing way?"

"Kokopelli travelled from village to village enchanting the young maidens with his song and his sexual favors. He tempted the maidens into following him back to the Kiva. The people mourned the loss of the maidens. They searched for them but could not find them. Kokopelli sent scouts in dreams to the sorcerers of the villages."

"Sorcerers." This was beginning to sound like a medieval fairy tale.

"The scouts guided the sorcerers to the Kiva in secret. When all of the sorcerers reached the Kiva, Kokopelli had the scouts take the maidens back to their villages and removed the spell from them. For many days Kokopelli taught the seeing way to the old ones. In honor of receiving this new knowledge, the sorcerers made the necklace for Kokopelli. Kokopelli blessed the necklace and placed it on the sipapu, the opening into the spirit world and the sacred altar of the Kiva. He warned them that if the knowledge was lost, they would not be able to mingle with the inorganic beings."

"What exactly are these inorganic beings?"

"To understand the inorganic beings, one must first understand the ways of the sorcerer, the Nagual. The sorcerer sees all the universe as energy flow. Everyone experiences the universe through the physical body and the energy body. The energy body exists as a companion to the physical body. It has substance but no physical matter. The inorganic beings have no physical body. They have only the energy body. But they have consciousness. For sorcerers, that is all that is needed for life."

"They're alive, but they don't have a body, a brain?" This was beginning to sound a little ridiculous.

"Consciousness is energy. When you become aware of the energy body and develop it, you can enter the energy flow through different entrances and exits, the seven gates, but you must learn how to use energy to develop the energy body. The sorcerer seeks to awaken the awareness of the energy body through dreaming. You begin by becoming aware of the dreaming attention. You can never enter the second attention without first entering the dreaming attention."

"How do you enter the dreaming attention?"

"When you become aware of the darkness and heaviness before deep sleep, you enter the dreaming attention. Then you have reached the first gate of dreaming."

"So, I simply know that I'm falling asleep, and I'm in the dreaming attention?"

"You must first set up the dream so that it doesn't become something different from what you intend. Think of something simple. Stare at an object. The dreaming attention waits for you to bring it into your awareness through intending to enter it."

"This is all getting very confusing."

"Do not let confusion overcome you. The inorganic beings will send scouts to feed on your confusion and lead you into tunnels where you will become lost forever. I will help you, but first you must understand the dangers of entering the second attention. The inorganic beings will try to keep you. They will send scouts, tempt you. They will offer you what you most desire. They can read your thoughts. They can project any image they wish at will. Only the experienced one can truly resist them."

"But how does one become experienced without actually entering the second attention?"

"If you resist the temptations of the inorganic beings, you will be approached by an emissary. She will help you find the way in and out. Do you have a gold ring?"

"No." Lesley wished now that she had taken the ring Jonathan had wanted to give her.

"Take this one." Pine Leaf takes a ring off her finger, hands it to Lesley. "The ring can act as a bridge back to the daily world. But it can also transport the wearer into the realm of the inorganic beings. It will attract energy you will need for the journey back. Take off your clothes. "

Lesley hesitates a moment, and then removes her clothes.

Pine Leaf gives Lesley a towel. "The skin must be cool and contain only your natural oils."

Lesley takes the towel and wipes down her body. She kneels again in front of the fire pit. Pine Leaf picks up the necklace and places it around Lesley's neck, positioning the pendant between her breasts. "Your skin and the necklace will help you use your energy from the daily world in the dream world. That energy will help you to return."

Pine Leaf moves back away from the fire. "When you encounter the inorganic beings, do not show fear. They feed off of fear. They can follow you back to the organic world if your fear is deep, and can drive you mad. They can be powerful allies or deadly adversaries. When they approach you, welcome them. Unite with them. They will want to join with you. They can show you tunnels that extend beyond the universe."

"How am I going to remember all of this?"

"You can return anytime you want. Remember the ring connects you with the daily world. The energy the ring collects will transport you back when you wish to leave. It's good the ring is tight. The Scouts will not be able to get it off your finger easily."

"You mean they might try to take the ring from me?"

"Yes. They need the energy of the ring as much as you do. Come and sit here with your back to me."

Lesley moves around the fire pit and sits in front of Pine Leaf.

"Stare into the fire and then close your eyes and take deep breaths. Concentrate your attention on seeing the fire. This is your point of departure into the dreaming attention. Do not let anything or anyone take your attention from the image of the fire. Observe the other contents of your dream in short looks, but return to the point of departure as often as you can." Lesley begins deep breathing. Suddenly, Pine Leaf slaps Lesley between the shoulder blades with her flattened hand.

The room turns black except for the glow of the fire pit. Lesley stares into it. She glances around the room, trying to pick out particular objects. The dim light from the fire hides anything that might be there. She stands up and slowly moves around the fire. A hint of light appears in front of her. She moves toward the light and sees the outline of a door. She opens the door and steps into a room that becomes her bedroom as a child. She quickly makes out objects from her childhood. A telescope. Her stuffed penguin, Penny. The book shelf with her "Boxcar Children" books. Photos of her family on her dresser. She stops at a photo of her brother, Conrad. The door to her closet slowly opens. Darkness inside, drawing her into it. She looks back at the fire pit. The darkness of the closet tugs at her. She sees herself approach the closet. Pine Leaf enters the room and grabs her arm.

"That can wait."

Lesley wants to enter the closet but goes with Pine Leaf. They move to a window and stand in front of it. Pine Leaf takes Lesley's hand.

"What do you see?"

Lesley speaks but her mouth doesn't move. "Birds. Trees. A stream. Blue sky. Clouds. The sun. People on a blanket beside the stream."

"Remember these." Pine Leaf pulls a shade. The window and Pine Leaf disappear. Lesley is engulfed in darkness.

The darkness opens up into a street, lively with people walking about. The people seem to know Lesley, greet her as she walks along. Lesley doesn't recognize any of them and walks along through the crowd. But to where? She tries to stop, but the crowd carries her forward. Lesley begins to panic, looks for any outlet to escape from the people. She spots an opening between two buildings ahead and darts in. The people don't seem to notice, continuing their hustle and bustle along the street.

Lesley watches from the inlet. Where was she? Was this part of the dream attention? She didn't like that she couldn't just leave. Or maybe she could. What was it Pine Leaf said to her? Return to the point of departure as often as you can. The fire. She had to think of the fire. The street and the people began to dissolve, and the fire appeared in front of Lesley. She could see herself sitting naked in front of the fire in the dark room in Pine Leaf's hogan.

"You have done well."

The voice didn't sound like Pine Leaf but was definitely female. It seemed to come from nowhere and everywhere around her, from inside her mind, from the fire, from the darkness.

"Look at the ring."

Lesley glanced at the ring on her finger. It glowed much brighter than what would have been produced from the dimness of the fire.

"You have collected enough energy to take you back to your world or to take you further into this world. You must choose which way you will go."

"How do I get where I want to go?"

"Just think of the place you want to be."

Lesley thought for a moment and then imagined herself in her condo back in New York. Nighttime. A rainstorm sent a constant torrent of raindrops against the wall of windows overlooking the Hudson. The room looked as if it had been redecorated, her furniture replaced with heavy, thick wooden pieces. Through the sound of the thunder of the storm, she could hear voices in the back room. She walked to the door and peeked in. On the bed she saw herself, naked, kneeling on top of someone, making love. Was that really the way she looked when making love? Or was this her idea of how she wanted to be when making love? She couldn't think of when she had been so "energetic" in her love-making, but the thought of it and the scene excited her. She wanted to know who had gotten this level of excitement out of her and moved around to see who her partner was. When she got close enough to see, a blinding light enveloped the room and knocked her back through the doorway.

She found herself brusquely transported to a desert-like setting with two strange, rubbery, luminous materializations directly in front of her. Lesley couldn't help feeling frightened by the creatures' appearances, tall, thin, wavering, with no real recognizable form. They seemed to be drawing energy from her and transmitting energy to her simultaneously. She knew that she shouldn't feel afraid, but what did they want with her? Why had they appeared at that exact moment in her dream? Too many unanswered questions filled Lesley's thoughts. All she wanted was to end this dream and get back to Pine Leaf. She thought again of her childhood bedroom and was instantly transported there.

Standing in her bedroom, she could see two doorways leading out. One engulfed in a bright white light; the other leading to darkness and the fire. She looked at the ring on her finger, the glow from the ring dimmer than what it had appeared before. She must have used a lot of energy on her last journey. Would she have enough to return if she didn't go back now.

A force pulled her through the doorway into the darkness and toward the fire. She saw herself sitting in front of the fire and felt the force guiding her to that spot. When she got to the spot, her dreaming form mingled with the sitting form to become one. She no longer saw herself but had become the figure she had seen. She looked again at the ring and concentrated on its glow. The light from the fire pit faded.

Lesley awoke on the floor by the fire pit. Pine Leaf remained in the same position as before.

Lesley's groggy. "Ohhh. What the hell happened? What did you do to me? I remember deep breathing and then everything went black."

"I used my energy to help you into the dreaming attention."

Was she dreaming or did she really travel somewhere else? "It felt like I was knocked out. My back is sore. Did I fall and hit something? How long was I unconscious?"

"You've been in the dreaming attention for a few hours."

"It seemed like only a few minutes. I thought I was going to find my father."

"You will, but the journey takes time."

"How long? I don't really have a lot of time for all of this."

"What do you remember?"

"Not much."

"Concentrate. What did you see?"

Lesley closes her eyes and tries to see the events of the dream. "Hmm. Well, I saw the fire pit. Then I was in my bedroom at home when I was a girl. The door to my closet opened. It was dark inside. I had a strong desire to enter the closet. Then you came into the dream and pulled me to a window. You know what I saw then."

"I was there with you and saw what I saw. What did you see?"

"A bright day. Blue sky and clouds. Trees, birds, a stream. Some people on a blanket by the stream."

"That is your place of refuge and belongs only to you. Mine is different. I saw none of that."

"What was in the closet?"

"Did you see the closet or did you see yourself seeing the closet?"

"I saw myself going toward the closet."

"That is good. You were being compelled by the inorganic beings. The closet was the second gateway. Once you see yourself in dream state, you are ready to move through the gateway to the second attention."

"Then I was in a street with a bunch of people who I didn't know, and I tried to get off the street and couldn't. Then I got pulled off and heard a voice I thought was you at first."

"What did the voice say?"

Lesley thinks for a moment. "It said I'd done well and told me I could either go on or go back. It told me to look at the ring."

"The emissary. The emissary can teach you and guide you where I can not."

"I saw I had enough energy to go on, so I thought of my place in New York. But everything was strange about it, like the street with all the people."

"That is because you have not crossed fully into the dream state yet. The more experienced you become, the less non-sensical your dreams will become."

"When I was at my place, I saw myself making love with someone, but I couldn't tell who it was. When I moved closer the room disappeared into a bright light and I was pulled away again. Why didn't I see who it was?"

"The Scouts wanted to tease you. As you become more accustomed to the dreaming attention, you will have the power to see others whom you will recognize."

"I don't want to see others. I just want to see my father."

"You have done well for your first visit. The spirit of the Earth Mother is strong in you. It will not take you long to discover the way. Come back tomorrow. Bring the necklace with you."

"One other thing. When I was pulled away by the light, I went into the desert and saw two large, thin creatures of pure light. They seemed to be connected to me."

"Those were elementals, inorganic beings who travel between the second attention and the daily world, like scouts, but more powerful. If you remain in the dream world, they will help you enter the third gate of dreaming. When the Bilaganna say that they have seen a ghost, they have seen an elemental. Now that they have contacted you, you can summon them even in your daily world. All you need do is close your eyes and see their form, and they will be with you."

"Why would I need to summon them in this world?"

"They can be helpful in returning to the second attention. They want to connect with you. That is good. Do not chase them away. If they appear in the daily world, grab a hold of them and don't let go."

Lesley dressed, gave the gold ring back to Pine Leaf, and left the hogan. The night had gotten cool, and she quickly started the engine on the Audi and grabbed a jacket from the back seat. She sat while the car warmed up and thought about the past few nights. Had she really gone into another state of being? The dream state felt real, but was that just the effect of the tea she had drank? What was in that tea anyway? One thing she knew for sure, she didn't know if she'd ever get used to being naked so much, especially in front of people she didn't know that well. It wasn't so bad with Pine Leaf, but the sweat lodge had been another story altogether, and she had to admit she had been excited by Alan. Was Alan the one she made love with? Should she do something about that? Right now she just wanted to get back to her room, take a nice long, hot bath and snuggle up in the bed. Alan said he would call that evening. Maybe she'd invite him over.

The drive back to town on the dark road lulled Lesley almost to sleep. She fought to keep her eyes open and tried listening to some up-tempo music. That helped some until she finally saw the lights of Cortez ahead and knew she'd be at the inn very soon.

She pulled into the inn, parked the car, and went straight to her room using the outside stairway. As soon as she entered the room she fell on the bed. That helped. Just a few minutes to relax, get up and undress and hit the bathtub. Almost ten o'clock. Probably a little late to be calling anyone, but the thought of the afternoon with Alan and the vision in her condo heated her blood. She'd jump in the bath before it got too late and then try Alan.

She peeled herself off of the bed, took off her shirt, slipped out of her jeans, and went to the bathroom. She wanted to wash some of the dust off first, and then she'd settle into the tub. She started the water for the tub, filled the sink with hot water, and tossed in a washcloth. The hot water in a motel always got hotter than at home. The hot washcloth soothed her face. Her skin shone bright red. She stared in the mirror at the Kokopelli necklace and the pendant dangling between her breasts. Sorcerers. Native

American spirits. Energy bodies. All of this sounded as fantastic as the stories about God and disciples and messiahs that she'd heard and read as a child. And this was just as real to Pine Leaf and David Nighteagle and Marianna as it was to the people who wrote and told those bible stories.

She splashed some water on her face, the excess trickling down over her breasts and onto the counter. She started to remove her panties when a shadow in the outer room caught her attention. She peeked into the outer room but saw nothing. Probably headlights from a car. She removed her panties, wrapped herself in a towel, and bent down to test the water in the tub. She stood up and felt a whoosh of wind behind her. Then, darkness.

10

neeznáá

****

Lesley strained to open her eyes. They resisted. The binding cut into her wrists and ankles as she twisted to try to move. No use. The tumult around her could easily have awakened the dead. She finally managed a slit to peer through. Was this a dream? She couldn't tell any more. Where was she? A room of some sort.

Smoke billowed from a huge fire in the middle of the room, wafting through the opening above it. Deafening drumming reverberated off the walls with a vast assortment of percussion instruments adding to the rhythm. Dancers circled the blaze in masks and ceremonial costume, chanting and singing along with the music. Old men crouched on the floor and on benches built into the walls, passing a pipe and a bowl of liquid from one to the other, each first sipping the liquid with an ornate spoon. Was this the Kiva they had found? If this was the Kiva she and Alan had discovered, it now appeared as it probably had a thousand years or more in the past and nothing like it had in the dim light earlier in the afternoon. Petroglyphs, pictographs, masks that had been hidden previously, filled niches and blanketed the walls of the fire-lit ceremonial room.

One main dancer resembling the Kokopelli image, conducted the ritual, ceremonial pipe in one hand, rattlesnake in the other, dancing among the gathering, circling a body on an altar in the Kiva center. The Kokopelli dancer wound around Lesley, lunged toward her, rattled the snake in her face, the Kokopelli necklace around the dancer's neck. The dancer returned to the body, pried open the snake's jaws, sprinkled venom on the body, placed the snake in a basket, lit the pipe, inhaled the smoke. The dancer then circled the body, using the pipe to mimic playing a flute.

A Hawk Shaman emerges from the crowd of dancers, hawk feathers covering both arms, a hawk mask completing the image. The Hawk Shaman dances around the body, imitating the movements of a hawk gliding on the airways of the canyons. Dips. Soars. Hawk screeching's blend with the din of the music and chanting.

The Kokopelli dancer removes the necklace and places it on the body, dips his hand into a bowl, scatters dust all around. The Hawk Shaman comes forward and places a Hawk feather on the body, mingles again with the other celebrants. The dancing becomes frenzied, the chanting a roar. More dancers appear wearing Hawk wings and masks. The pounding of the drums shakes the Kiva walls. Lesley desperately tries to loosen her bonds but merely irritates the now raw skin of her wrists and ankles. She tries to look away but cannot, drawn inescapably to the event, the smoke and heat adding to the intoxication.

The revelers open a huge circle around the altar, continue the chanting and dancing. The body slowly ascends into the air, hovering, motionless. The Kokopelli dancer now circles the body, dips into a medicine bag tied around its waist, sprinkles dust onto the fire. A smoky haze envelops the dancer and the body. Lesley can barely make out the figure, and then the haze clears somewhat.

A transformation begins. Arms and legs of the body withdraw into the clothing, replaced by wings and talons. The head morphs, nose becoming a beak, hair giving way to sleek feathers. The clothing falls away, the body now resembling an enormous hawk. The Hawk stands regally in the middle of the circle, while a huge, shadowy Kokopelli figure appears in the smoke. Dancing and chanting has now reached a fever pitch. Lesley screams! But her screams melt into the din of the chamber. The Kokopelli figure dissolves into the air, the Hawk emits an ear-splitting shriek, shrinks to normal size, shoots into the air, orbits the fire, disappears through the Kiva opening. The Kokopelli dancer lifts the necklace from the altar, replaces the necklace around his neck, continues the ceremony, chanting, drumming, ecstatic dancing.

Lesley tries to make sense of what she's just seen. Her mind races, filled with the images from her dreaming journey and now. Could she have entered the dreaming attention somehow? Was she in a tunnel opened to her by a scout? Had Pine Leaf done something else to her? Her mind couldn't take any more, the dizzying bombardment, the heat, the frenzy, the roar. Darkness began to overtake her.

The Kokopelli dancer approaches Lesley, removes the necklace, kneels and puts the necklace around Lesley's neck, positioning the pendant between her breasts. Through the ceremonial paint and guise, the face looks hauntingly familiar. Bold Sun? She tries to speak but can't muster the energy. A faint "You?" escapes her lips. The elements take their toll on her, and she blacks out.

****

Shrieks from a Hawk cascade over the canyon walls. Lesley awakens, nestled on a blanket on an outcrop of a cliff, baking in the mid-morning sun. She closes her eyes, waits a minute until she feels more awake, sits up. She scans the area. How the hell did she get up here? She stands up and shakily moves as close as she dare to the edge of the outcrop. Several hundred foot drop below. Steep cliffs all around her. Ruins of small Pueblo dwellings scattered along the canyon walls. She sees her bag next to a rock, rummages through it, finds a water bottle and guzzles almost half of it. No phone. She grabs a t-shirt and bandana and covers herself. She struggles through hazy recollection to piece together the events of the night. Images flash through her mind. Kiva walls. Dancers. Kokopelli. A hawk. A huge hawk. Bold Sun? How did she end up here? How could anyone have even gotten here, carried her, to leave her behind?

Lesley takes another swig on the water and examines the sides of the outcrop. On one side, a solid wall of rock without any obvious ways of climbing above or below. On the other side, some striation that could allow climbing. Then she notices some small notches that appear to be carved into the stone wall, leading up, too tiny to fit her foot into with her shoes on. Man-made? She removes her shoes and socks, sticks them inside her bag. Her feet immediately feel the sting of the sun's rays. She splashes a small pool of the water onto the dirt, mixes it with the dirt, and rubs the mud onto her feet. She takes one more look down to the bottom of the canyon floor and up above. About thirty feet to the top of the wall. Damn. At least the wall had a slight incline instead of being straight up. This would still take all the energy she could muster. She wraps the bag around her shoulder and starts the arduous climb, notices the hawk circling over the crest of the canyon.

Her feet and hands fit snuggly into the notches, scraping slightly the skin on her fingers and toes. She moves slowly, a few moves at a time, the rocks tearing her skin on her stomach and chest. Knowing that looking down wouldn't be a good thing, she keeps her attention on the few feet above her, stopping every few notches to rest. Even with the breaks, she begins feeling faint from the heat and the exertion. Maybe she should have waited a little longer before trying this.

The sun bakes her. She needed her hat. Her thoughts begin to wander. Looking up, she envisions images of Conrad from earlier in life calling her to climb up. "Come on, Lesley!. Dad's waiting for us! Hurry!" She struggles to maintain her grip. Blood stains the rock wall. She slips, catches herself, pauses to rest. The Hawk circles over head, it's shrieks calling to her. "Lesley!" "Lesley!" Conrad now becomes the Hawk Shaman, lunges at Lesley from above. She winces, hugs the wall, shuts her eyes. Pine Leaf appears, her words calm Lesley. "The spirit of the Earth Mother is strong in you."

Lesley spots the Hawk. Her thoughts return to her fall from years before. The Hawk flying above her. Her safe landing on the ledge. Her dad leaning over her. "Lesley? Les. You'll be okay." His final words echo in her mind. "You'll be okay. You'll be okay. You'll be okay . . . ." She catches a second wind, digs her fingers into the wall, climbs with more energy. Near the top she slips, dangles, tosses the strap from her bag around a rock, pulls herself up. She clears the top, tumbles to the ground, savors the feel of solid earth. After a few moments of rest, she sits up, struggles to put on her shoes, stands,. The Hawk circles one last time and sails across the landscape. Lesley follows the direction of the Hawk, each step she takes reminding her of the raw skin on the bottoms of her feet.

****

About mid-afternoon, an old pickup truck pulls up to the Turquoise Inn. Lesley hauls herself out of the passenger side, dragging her bag across the seat. A rotund Navajo woman sits in the driver's seat. Little kids in the back of the pickup wave and scream to Lesley. She waves back.

The woman calls after her. "You be okay, hon?"

"I'll be fine. Thank you for the lift."

"You get something on those cuts before they get infected. Get some cactus juice."

"I will. Thanks again."

"Hágoónee!"

"Yes, Hágoónee."

The children scream and wave. "Hágoónee! Hágoónee!"

Lesley tries to muster some energy to respond. "Hágoónee!" She shuts the door, painfully walks into the motel. The desk clerk stops her.

"Ms. Whitney. Sheriff's been looking for you. Was worried. Couldn't get you on your phone. You okay?"

Should she report what happened to the desk clerk, that someone had gotten into her room and kidnapped her? She'd save her energy for when she talked with the sheriff. "I just need a shower and a nap, in that order. Did the sheriff say what he wanted?"

"Said he'd try to reach you this afternoon. Had some information for you. I've got a first aid kit here if you need anything."

"That would be great."

Lesley takes the first aid kit, uses the elevator this time, trudges the rest of the way to her room, each step draining a little more of her nearly exhausted energy. She slips into the room, immediately removes her clothes, sinks into the tub with the shower pouring over her. Should she tell the sheriff what happened to her? He'd surely ask. Would he believe her was the question. Would anyone believe she saw what she thought she saw. She didn't imagine waking up on the side of the cliff, climbing to the top, hitch-hiking back to the inn. But what about the rest of it?   All of that thinking would have to wait. She just wanted now to relax. She settled into the tub, the water pounding her skin, easing her tension, soothing her aching muscles. She drifts.

****

The cold water from the shower shocked Lesley awake. How long had she been in there? She'd never known hot water in a motel bathroom to turn cold. She turned off the water, wrapped a towel around, and went into the outer room, checked her phone. Eight missed calls. One from Columbia. Probably Elliot calling to check on her. Two from Jonathan. She'd get back to him later. Three from Sheriff Branshee. She needed to call him first. One from Alan. Hmm. Interesting. And one from, Shanee? Wonder what she wanted. She'd call her after she talked with the sheriff.

She called down to the front desk and ordered a turkey club. About three times more for it from room service, but her stomach reminded her that she hadn't eaten in over fourteen hours. The sandwich would last her until dinner. Maybe she'd get Alan to take her to Mama Rosa's again before going to Pine Leaf's. Could she even do that this evening? Pine Leaf expected her, so she needed to be there.

She'd return the Sheriff's call while she waited for the club, get dressed, and make a run out to the center. Wondering what Shanee wanted nagged at her.

11

lá'ts'áadah

****

The turkey club had taken longer than Lesley had expected, and now the afternoon traffic slowed her drive to the center. Shanee would be there until five. Alan had been out with a group and didn't answer her call. She'd talked with the Sheriff, finally, after the woman at the office tracked him down. Something about a battery.

"I just wanted to let you know that the body we found in the canyon wasn't your father. We still don't know who it was. Maybe some old prospector got trapped in a flash flood in one of the gulches. But we know it's not the Doc. It was almost a foot shorter than him."

"I don't think my father is in the canyon anyway."

"Why do you say that?"

"We found the site he'd been searching for."

"We?"

"Alan, Dr. Hall, found a map dad had left at the center in with some of his stuff. We followed it to the site up in the canyon. You wouldn't find it without the map."

"Did you search the place?"

"We looked around some and didn't see any signs that anyone had been there. But I was there again last night."

"What were you doing up there last night?"

"I'm still trying to figure that out myself."

"I don't understand."

"Me either, but I think Bold Sun had something to do with it."

"Why do you say that?'

"I think he was there too."

"Sounds pretty strange, Dr. Whitney."

"I know. I would like to be able to talk with him just to reassure myself."

"He sometimes stays at a farm that his organization runs outside of town. Don't know if you'd find him there though. Kinda hard to keep up with him."

"I can believe that."

"You need me to do anything?"

"No. I just wanted to talk with him."

"Looks like we're back to square one with the Doc. Sorry I don't have any better news for you. We'll keep lookin' though. I'll keep in touch. Let me know if you need anything."

"I will sheriff. And thank you."

She turned onto the dirt road that led to the center, Mesa Verde towering in the distance. A jackrabbit scurried across the road in front of her, dove into the brush, disappeared as quickly as it had hopped into view. Approaching the center, Lesley noticed Alan standing out by the vehicle shed, talking and joking with two young Navajo men seated in a souped up, black Bronco. Alan didn't notice as she drove by. The driver revved the engine on the Bronco and peeled out, raising a cloud of dust. Alan drove off toward the Pueblo Learning Center in one of the

Coyote Canyon vans. Lesley parked in front of the lodge, walked to the main building to meet with Shanee.

Shanee waited for her in the lobby, greets Lesley. "Thanks for coming out, Lesley."

"It's okay. I was actually hoping you could help me with something. But you go first."

"Sure. Let's sit." She leads Lesley to the secluded corner with the very comfy Southwestern style furniture.

As they sit, Shanee produces a letter. "I found this the other day in with some of Arthur's things at my place. I guess he thought I'd eventually find it. I knew you'd want to see it."

Lesley unfolds the letter, reads to herself, hearing Arthur's voice speak the words.

My Dearest Shanee,

These past months have been some of the most fascinating of my life. Meeting you has especially been the most exhilarating experience. You remind me so much of my daughter, Lesley. Your exuberance. Your curiosity. Your zest for life. Those are some of her finest qualities. I really wish the two of you could meet. We haven't talked in years, though, and I don't even know if she would want to talk with me now. It's too difficult to explain in a letter, but maybe I'll tell you about it some day. Just know that you have been a primal force in reenergizing my life. I hope that we will have much more time to spend with each other.

Yours,

Arthur

Lesley folds the letter and gives it back to Shanee, fights to hold back the tears from welling up in her eyes.

"Can I ask you something?"

Lesley nods "yes."

"I told you Arthur missed you very badly, regretted not having seen you in years."

"That's not a question."

Shanee grins. "Okay, then. Why had you not talked to Arthur for so long?"

"I'm not surprised he didn't tell you. He didn't talk about Conrad after the accident."

"Conrad?"

"My brother. This isn't my first time here. We were exploring with dad. I was only eight. Conrad was fourteen. We were climbing up to a cliff house. Conrad fell trying to help me. Broke his neck. It left him a paraplegic. Then he developed epilepsy. Mom and I had to take care of him. Dad couldn't stand to be around after that. He blamed me. I felt guilty and closed everyone out. Didn't want to face mom and dad after that. I spent my time taking care of Conrad."

"I can't believe Arthur would just leave you like that."

"He always pushed so hard for us to be strong. To be like him. Especially Conrad. I think he just didn't want to see Conrad like that and not be able to fix things. So, I guess in the end we were the strong ones."

"I know it seems like Arthur didn't care, but you know what guilt can do to a person. Makes you do crazy things."

"But there's no way I would ever abandon my child, especially when he needed my support the most."

"He stayed away after that?"

"Oh, he came around sometimes. Sent money. Took care of expenses, college, all that. He was everything but there. That's how, that's why, I studied medicine. I wanted to do something to help Conrad."

"Who's taking care of Conrad now?"

"He and my mother were killed in an auto accident four years ago. Dad never even showed up for the funeral."

"He probably felt helpless or thought his presence would torture him and you about the accident. He would never give up on you."

"And I won't give up on him till I know the truth."

Shanee changes the subject. "You said I could help you with something."

"I want to get in touch with someone. Bold Sun. The sheriff said he sometimes stays at a farm around here. Do you know him or where this farm is?"

"Everybody around here knows who Bold Sun is. He's pretty mysterious. Comes and goes as he pleases. Works with the Navajo Nation sometimes. They tend to distance themselves from him though. He has a more radical approach than they want to project."

"Can we get in touch with him somehow?"

"I can give you directions to the farm. Better yet, why don't I just take you out there." Shanee gets up. "Do you have time right now?"

Lesley gets up. "Let's go."

****

The farmhouse looked deserted, like it hadn't been inhabited for years. Windows covered with dust. Everything covered with dust. Plants grew wildly all around the different buildings on the property. Cactus, sage ran rampant. No animals that one would normally see on a farm. Ostriches in an enclosed area next to the barn. Odd.

Lesley parks in front of the farmhouse, a two-story Colonial. She and Shanee get out. Shanee walks to the porch while Lesley surveys the area. On the porch, Shanee knocks on the door. Lesley walks to the side of the house, looks around, in windows. She tries to clean off the grime enough to see in. No use. The wail of a peacock breaks the silence, startles Lesley. Shanee peers from the porch. Grins at Lesley. Lesley continues to patrol the side and back of the house, ostriches parade in the corral by the barn. Lesley moves to the barn, peers in the barn doors. Empty. She turns back toward the house. Inside the house, unseen by Lesley and Shanee, a hand scarcely opens the curtain in an upstairs window.

Lesley stands below. A strong wind whips dust in the air, encircling Lesley. She's held fast, tries to move. Can't. The wind increases. In the swirl of dust, Lesley makes out the figures of the elementals. She remembers Pine Leaf's words: If they appear in the daily world, grab a hold of them and don't let go. She lurches forward and wraps her arms around one of the figures, feels a surge of electricity pulsating through her. She and the elemental tangle, twist and jostle about, the electrical pulses continuing, not stronger, just constant. They remain in their wrestling match, the electricity from the creature causing Lesley to react with an animalistic intensity. After a few moments, the elemental quits squirming and lies still, Lesley resting on top of it.

Without warning, instantaneously, the wind stops. Lesley lies motionless on the ground. Only the continued wailing of the peacocks pierces the air. Shanee now catches sight of Lesley sprawled on the ground, runs to her. She kneels beside her, helps Lesley sit up.

"What the hell?"

Lesley's caked with dust, spits and coughs dust from inside her, still feeling agitated from the electrical charges. Shanee helps brush her off. Lesley jumps up, stumbles, shouts to the sky. "Damnit!" She stands still, bends over, straightens up. "Shit!"

"Someone doesn't want you around here."

Lesley clears her throat. "I'd have never guessed that."

Shanee helps Lesley to the front porch. They sit on the steps. "You okay?" Lesley nods. Shanee gets water from the car and brings it back to Lesley. "Can you get my bag from the car?"

Shanee gets the bag, brings it back. Lesley pulls out paper and a pencil.

"What are you writing?"

"A note to Bold Sun. If I can't talk to him, maybe he'll get the note." Lesley finishes, folds the note, pushes it through the mail slot in the front door. "Do you have a four wheel drive?"

"No. Pickup." They get in the car.

"Drop me off at Pine Leaf's, then go to Alan and get him to let you use his."

"That Land Rover is his baby. He doesn't let anyone touch it."

"Do what you have to do. Just get it."

****

Firelight glistens over Lesley's naked body under the star-filled sky, the yellow-tinted light reflecting off of the Kokopelli necklace between Lesley's breasts. Pine Leaf prepares tea at the fire pit, finishes a sand painting circle next to the blaze. She opens a section of the circle, beckons Lesley.

"Sit here in the middle of the circle."

Lesley moves to the circle, kneels in the center. "I had an encounter with the elementals earlier. I grabbed one like you said. It kept shocking me with these electrical charges, and then it just stopped and lay still."

"You drained it of its energy. You have now made a connection with them."

Pine Leaf pours tea into a cup, gives Lesley the cup. "You have seen what very few have seen. This will be of great service to you."

"Drink this."

Lesley sips at the tea.

"You must drink all of it."

Lesley finishes the tea, hands the cup to Pine Leaf. Pine Leaf gives Lesley the gold ring. Lesley places it on her finger. Pine Leaf gets up and begins chanting, dancing around Lesley. Lesley starts getting dizzy, sees Pine Leaf dancing around her in slow motion. Pine Leaf slaps Lesley on the back with her open hand.

The fire pit disappears. Darkness overcomes Lesley. A series of light filaments course through the air. Whisperings, whooshes of wind.. The filaments become brighter, more abundant, swirling throughout. The whooshing's and whisperings become deafening. A dark spot opens in front of Lesley, engulfing the light filaments. The spot grows. Filaments combine. A bright orb forms. Lesley glides in the direction of the orb, as if floating, until surrounded by light.

Brilliant light bursts into strands, trails of light shoot everywhere. Light beams emit from Lesley's form, attach to certain strands, shoot parallel to them, dancing with them. A series of tunnels form in front of Lesley. A female voice, the Emissary, speaks.

"Your journey lies through the tunnels."

Lesley speaks without moving her lips. "Which tunnel?"

"You will know."

"How do I know this isn't a trick?"

"Trust your instincts."

Mirror-like images now appear. Lesley becomes a strand of light, flitters back and forth across the mirror images. She reflects off one of the images, enters darkness, regains human form, the maze of tunnels before her. Images appear in the tunnels.

Alan appears at the entrance to one. Lesley sees herself with Alan, both naked. They embrace. Alan kisses her. She responds. Alan's hands course over Lesley's body. She kisses him feverishly, explores his body. Alan ends the kiss. Grabs Lesley by the hand. "Lesley, Arthur's in here. I'll take you to him." He tries to pull Lesley into the tunnel. She breaks free. The image dissolves.

Another tunnel opens. Jonathan appears. "Just let me help you, Lesley. I can help you." He waves for Lesley to follow. She resists. The tunnel closes.

Elliot Mueller appears at a different tunnel entrance. "Lesley. Follow me. Arthur's right inside. He sent me to get you. Trust me." Behind the image, Lesley catches a glimpse of a shadowy being. The shadow zooms down the tunnel, the entrance closes.

Then Arthur appears in a tunnel. "Lesley! I'm in here! Help me!" The image begins fading back into the tunnel, as if being pulled backwards. "Don't let them take me, Lesley?"

Lesley senses a strong attraction to the image, sees herself moving toward the tunnel, nearing the image, like drawn to a magnet. The image recedes further into the tunnel, beckoning, a look of agony on its face. A dread rush overcomes Lesley. She tries to back away from the tunnel. The image responds, moves toward Lesley now. Lesley scurries out of the tunnel as it collapses, the image dissolving into the darkness.

Finally, Conrad appears at the entrance to a tunnel. He's the Conrad that Lesley remembers from before the accident. "Les. Dad's in here. He's waiting for us. He wants to see us. Come on." He moves into the tunnel, waving Lesley to follow, stands and waits for her, smiling.

Conrad's tunnel attracts Lesley. As she moves closer, she's gently pulled toward the tunnel by shadow-like beings, drawing her closer and closer to the tunnel entrance, the more she resists the stronger they pull. The beings clamor to pull her closer, more beings appearing by the second. The beings begin assuming different forms, warped images of Lesley, negative images, transparent images of people she has encountered, whom she knows. The beings completely surround Lesley, a distorted tangle of shapes, forms. Lesley relaxes, ceases resisting the beings. They swarm around her, caressing her body, penetrating her aura, immersing Lesley in an orgasmic ecstacy.

In the midst of the clamor, the elementals appear. The shadow beings revert to their original form, begin evaporating, releasing their hold on Lesley, scurry into various tunnels. She reappears at the entrance to the tunnel maze. Strands appear again, dart everywhere, form a huge orb of light. Lesley's ring shines in the brilliance of the light, lured to the ball. The glow of the ring devours Lesley's body, merges with the ball of light. The light expands, bursts into a thousand strands. Blackness.

The fire rages in the fire pit, stoked by the desert wind, casts a glow on Pine Leaf and Lesley. Lesley lies in the circle, Pine Leaf kneels over her, brushes her hair aside, washes her face with a cloth, places a blanket on her. Pine Leaf sits next to the fire, gazing into the flames.

Shanee appears out of the darkness, rushes to Lesley. "Is she okay?"

"She is resting. She will be fine."

"When can I talk to her?"

"She will awaken soon. Come. Here. Sit."

Shanee kneels beside Pine Leaf at the fire. They both stare into the flames.

As the morning emerges, rays of sunlight dance across the horizon. Flames from the fire gently hug the logs. Shanee reclines against a rock by the fire, sleeping. Pine Leaf sits upright, eyes shut, motionless. Lesley begins to stir, opens her eyes, stares above. Momentarily, she looks around, sees Shanee and Pine Leaf. She nudges Shanee awake.

"Shh."

Shanee wakes, slowly raises up, massages her arms. "Hey. How are you doing?"

"I'm fine. Come on."

"What about Pine Leaf?"

"She'll be back later."

"What?"

"Just come on."

B. R. Fleming

12

naakits'áadah

****

The sun peeked over the La Plata Range, began the task of warming the earth. Lesley maneuvered Alan's Land Rover over a narrow road, now managing to drink her coffee and navigate the vehicle. Shanee sipped coffee in the passenger seat.

"I still can't believe you wrangled this puppy from Alan."

A grin spreads across Shanee's lips. "It's going to cost you later."

The road abruptly turned from asphalt to dirt, becoming bumpier, narrower, climbing further into the mountains. Lesley continued, unfazed, finished her coffee, tossed the cup in the back seat, jammed the gearshift into a lower gear, repositioned herself for the more intense driving conditions. Shanee glued her feet onto the dash, hanging on.

An hour later, the sun shone brightly. Deer grazed on brush on the side of the cliffs. Rabbits scurried across the landscape. Lesley and Shanee had removed the doors of the

Land Rover and their jackets. The road had smoothed out somewhat. Shanee held a topographic map in her lap.

Lesley had to almost yell to be heard over the sound of the wind, the Land Rover, and the road. "Dad knew how important the Kiva was. I think he came back to search for more evidence. When did you last see him?"

Shanee hesitates a moment. "He stayed with me the night before he left."

Lesley hesitates now. "Did he tell you why he wanted to keep the Kiva a secret?"

"He said that it was very sacred ground. That it shouldn't be disturbed.

"Why didn't he tell Alan about it? Weren't they working together? Sort of."

"He was going to tell him when he returned. I don't think they really worked together that closely."

Lesley thinks for a moment. "What would you say if I told you dad wasn't lost?"

"I'd say, 'where is he then?'"

"He may be dead. He may be hiding. He may be on a journey into the second attention."

"I'd say, 'I want some of those Peyote buttons you've been popping.'"

The Land Rover squeals to a halt. Lesley points to a dirt road.

"Isn't that the way to the Kiva?"

"Yes. We keep going straight ahead to get to the camp." Lesley shoves the gearshift into first and takes off. The vehicle bumps and grinds through a mostly dried up creek bed. Thick brush, Mesquite line the creek bed.

"We should be getting close now."

"Looks like the brush is thinning out ahead."

Vegetation slowly gives way to dirt and rocks. The high desert. Canyon walls grow on each side of the pass. The

Land Rover rolls around a bend. Ahead, a series of tributary canyons intersect the larger Lost Canyon route. At the mouth of one, Lesley spots a black Bronco, grinds the Land Rover to a halt.

"That looks like the Bronco I saw at the center."

"What would they be doing up here?"

"Let's find out."

Lesley parks the Rover behind an outcrop. They grab backpacks and water bottles, set out toward the Bronco. As they approach, Lesley signals to Shanee to keep things quiet. They sneak around to the Bronco, check out the interior, find nothing.

"They must be up this trail."

"Arthur's camp is up there."

"What do you think? Should we call the sheriff?"

"Probably wouldn't get reception up here." Shanee reaches in her backpack, pulls out a revolver.

Lesley's surprised. "Can you use that?"

Shanee loads bullets into the pistol. "I've been known to tag a rattler on occasion."

Lesley starts up the trail. Shanee follows. The passage wends its way into the canyon, dense brush and Mesquite forming as they move further. About a quarter mile in, voices can be heard.   Lesley and Shanee cautiously approach, hide behind some rocks, watch in a clearing at a campsite as two young Navajo men pack backpacks, trade tokes on a joint.

Shanee whispers. "This is Arthur's campsite."

Lesley recognizes the two men. "Those are the two guys I saw Alan talking with at the center."

"I know who they are. The taller one is Yellow Horse. The other one's Silk Shirt. At least that's what they go by. Their names are Eddie Pinto and Tommy Dashee. They do work for the center sometimes. I think they were bringing supplies to Arthur when he stayed up here."

Yellow Horse takes a toke on the joint and passes it to Silk Shirt. "Man, you know there's nothing left of that old fuck by now."

Silk Shirt takes a long toke on the joint. "Got no choice. Now the sheriff and his men have quit snoopin', he wants us to make sure."

"Sheriff didn't even find anything. How's anybody else gonna find that old Bilaganna."

"So, you sayin' we should just tell 'im we checked. Leave it at that."

"How the fuck's he gonna know any different?"

Silk Shirt passes the joint back to Yellow Horse. "Five years from now, some fucker's up here fuckin' around, finds some bones, takes 'em back to the sheriff. Investigation reopened. Then what?"

Yellow Horse shrugs.

"That's what I thought. Get that stuff packed, dickhead."

Yellow Horse takes a toke on the joint, hands it back to Silk Shirt, continues packing the backpack.

Lesley slumps to the ground. "You think they were talking about dad?"

"Why would they kill him? Nothing he would have had up here would have been worth killing him for."

"Alan said the site would be an important find. And they might have been looking for this." She pulls the Kokopelli necklace out from her shirt.

Shanee stares at the piece. "That's beautiful. But it couldn't be worth enough to kill someone."

"It's ancient. A very sacred object. Dad sent it to me for safe-keeping."

"I doubt they would even know anything about it. What do you want to do?"

"I want to find out who the old Bilaganna was they were talking about."

"You don't want to just tell the sheriff and let him handle it?"

Lesley stuffs the necklace in her pants pocket, glares at Shanee.

Shanee pulls out the revolver. "Let's go."

Lesley and Shanee move out from behind the rocks and into the clearing. Shanee cocks the hammer on the pistol. Silk Shirt and Yellow Horse hear the hammer click, react. Silk Shirt goes for a rifle, Yellow Horse grabs for his high tech crossbow.

"Don't do it!" Shanee aims the revolver at them. Lesley stands next to her.

Silk Shirt stops a few feet from the rifle. "We was just borrowin' some supplies. Didn't mean no harm. We'll go."

"Yeah, we was just goin'." Yellow Horse inches toward the crossbow.

"Not yet."

Shanee waives the revolver at them. "Just stay right where you are." She motions for Lesley to continue.

"Who sent you up here?"

Yellow Horse sneers. "Nobody sent us. We was just--"

Silk Shirt interrupts Yellow Horse. "We just came to do some hikin'. Any problem with that?"

"Then what was all that talk about bones being found and the sheriff?"

"Sacred bones. That's what we do when we're hikin'. Search for bones and stuff."

Shanee breaks in. "They're pot hunters. They rob the sites and sell the stuff to museums through the black market."

"We don't rob nothin'!" Silk Shirt motions for Yellow Horse to be quiet. Yellow Horse inches closer toward his crossbow.

Silk Shirt tries to draw their attention to him. "The stuff'll just get stolen by the Bilaganna. At least we can make a little bit of a living off it."

"You can make a living some other way. Go to school. Get a job."

"Like you? Work for the Bilaganna for little a nothing at Coyote Canyon?"

"It beats going to jail."

"At least in there we get three squares and all the dope we want. It ain't so bad." Yellow Horse inches closer.

"Is that what you were doing at the center? Trying to sell artifacts?

"We do some work for 'em. Nothing illegal."

Lesley pulls out her cell phone. "Maybe we should let the sheriff ask the questions." She punches numbers into the phone. Nothing.

Shanee glances at the phone screen. "I told you it probably wouldn't work up here."

"How would dad have contacted anyone?" Silk Shirt and Yellow Horse trade glances.

Shanee looks around. "Must be a radio somewhere."

Lesley moves closer toward the camp. Yellow Horse dives, grabs the crossbow, rolls, fires at Shanee, hitting her in the hand. Shanee drops the revolver. Lesley goes for it.

"Leave it!" Silk Shirt now has his rifle aimed at them. Lesley goes to Shanee, crouching on the ground holding her hand, pulls a bandana from her pocket, wraps Shanee's hand. Yellow Horse reloads the crossbow, aims at them.

"Now we ask the questions."

Yellow Horse grins. "Yeah, we ask the questions."

"Shut the fuck up. Get that fuckin' pistol." Yellow Horse grabs the pistol, tosses it by the backpack.

Shanee whispers to Lesley. "Sorry. What now?"

"I don't know. I'm thinking."

"What're you two doin' up here spyin' on us?"

Lesley keeps quiet. Silk Shirt moves toward her.

"When I ask a question, I want an answer." He roughly pulls Lesley up.

"What're you doin' here?" Lesley struggles. Silk Shirt holds tighter.

"Been a while since I had a Bilaganna girl." Silk Shirt scans Lesley's body. He holds out the rifle. Yellow Horse grabs it, trains it on them. Silk Shirt holds Lesley's arms around her back and runs his hand over her breasts, rips open her shirt. Yellow Horse watches excitedly. Silk Shirt thrusts his hand into Lesley's bra, clutches a breast. Lesley struggles harder but is no match for Silk Shirt.

Shanee screams at Silk Shirt. "Stop it! We just came to look at a site."

"Shut the fuck up, bitch!" Silk Shirt continues rubbing Lesley's breasts.

"I work at the center. We have a new site up here we're digging."

"Nobody digs up here. Ain't nothin' to dig."

"We found a new site. We're trying to get a permit."

Yellow Horse rubs his crotch. "That musta been what that old Bilaganna was doin'."

Silk Shirt throws Lesley down, yanks the rifle from Yellow Horse's grip, knocks Yellow Horse to the ground. Lesley scrambles to Shanee, covers herself with the ripped shirt. Yellow Horse grabs the crossbow.

Silk Shirt points the rifle at Yellow Horse. "You stupid shithead!"

Yellow Horse points the crossbow at Silk Shirt. "What the fuck!"

Lesley collects herself. "What did you do to my father?"

"Now you see dickhead." Silk Shirt turns the rifle on Lesley and Shanee again. Yellow Horse gets up.

"Now we gotta do something with 'em."

Yellow Horse lays the crossbow on a rock. "I got a good idea."

"What happened to my father?"

Silk Shirt grins. "It's what the sheriff's gonna call a tragic accident."

"Come on man, I got a boner goin'."

"Make it quick. We got a meeting to make."

Yellow Horse drops the crossbow, starts for Lesley. Lesley scrambles to her feet, starts to run. Yellow Horse jumps, pulls Lesley down.

Shanee tries to pull Yellow Horse off. "Leave her alone!"

Silk Shirt thrusts the rifle in Shanee's face. Yellow Horse and Lesley struggle. Yellow Horse slaps her, pins her, rips off the torn shirt. He buries his face in her breasts. Lesley pulls his hair, tries to pull his face away. He sits up, slaps her again. She's numb. Silk Shirt laughs.

Yellow Horse sits on Lesley's chest, his crotch in her face, starts to unzip his pants. "You ever tasted horse meat, little Bilaganna?" He laughs. Lesley strains to get out from under him.

A shot rings out. Yellow Horse collapses in pain onto Lesley. Lesley screams, pushes Yellow Horse off, scurries away. Silk Shirt pivots with the rifle, looking for the shooter.

A voice comes from the rocks behind Silk Shirt. "Everybody freeze." Silk Shirt freezes. Alan moves from behind the rocks holding a rifle, walks toward the camp. Shanee hurries over to Lesley. Alan stops behind Silk Shirt.

"Put the gun down. Slow." Silk Shirt reacts, starts to turn, relaxes his grip on the rifle

"What the fuck--" Alan clobbers Silk Shirt with the butt end of the rifle. Silk Shirt sinks to the ground. Alan moves to Lesley and Shanee. Lesley crouches on the ground trying to cover herself, still shaken from Yellow Horse's attack. Shanee holds onto her.

"Whatever the hell you're doing here, I'm really glad you showed up."

Alan bends down to check on Lesley. "I sure didn't expect to find you like this. What the hell are you two doing up here anyway? You said you were just going to look around."

"We were just looking around when we saw their black Bronco at the mouth of this canyon. We were wondering what they were doing around Arthur's camp. Do you know them?"

"I know who they are. They've done some work for Barry and for the center. I've talked with them a few times. But just joking around kind of stuff."

Lesley stares out. "I think they killed dad."

"Why do you say that?"

"They were talking about an old guy and hiding bones when we came up. And I think your boss might have hired them to get dad out of the way."

"Barry? He's pretty opportunistic when it comes to the center. But murder?"

"Dad didn't want to disturb the Kiva. Barry probably knew about it. And these two were talking about some meeting they had with someone."

Shanee let's go of Lesley, starts to get up. "That's right. Just before his last trip up here, Arthur told me he didn't want Barry to find out about it yet. He wanted to do a little more exploring around the area first."

"That sounds like dad. The only great Kiva found in this remote area. And the only one found in over one hundred years. That would bring a lot of prestige for the center."

Shanee helps Lesley up. "Not to mention research dollars."

"We'll let the sheriff figure all this out. Let's get you two back to town."

Lesley glares at Yellow Horse and Silk Shirt. "What about them?"

"I'll take care of them. You two go on down to the Land Rover and wait for me."

Lesley and Shanee hobble away. Alan goes to Yellow Horse, checks his pulse. He's half conscious. He goes to Silk Shirt, turns him over. Silk Shirt moans. Alan slaps him. Silk Shirt stirs, opens his eyes, still groggy from the blow.

"What the fuck're you doin' shootin' my blood brother?"

"If you two would have just done what I said, none of this would have happened."

"We were gonna take care of it. Then they showed up." Alan pulls Silk Shirt up.

"You're gonna jump me and get Yellow Horse and get out of here. Go and make sure no evidence is left. Then take off for a while. Come and find me when you get back."

"Yeah. You should be famous by then." Alan turns around. Silk Shirt pops him with his rifle butt. Alan slumps to the ground.

In the back seat of the Land Rover, Lesley just sits and stares out, deep in thought. Shanee sits in the front seat, checks the trail, checks her watch.

"What's taking Alan so long?" She glances up the trail again. "I'm gonna go check on him."

Lesley jumps out. "I'll go. Lesley hikes back to the camp.

Lesley reaches the camp, hides behind some brush, sees Alan on the ground and Silk Shirt packing his back pack.

She moves to get a closer look. Silk Shirt hides the backpacks in some brush, picks up Yellow Horse, balances him on his shoulder, starts to move toward the trail. Lesley spots Silk Shirt's rifle and the crossbow. She moves closer. Silk Shirt reaches to pick up the rifle. Lesley snatches up the crossbow, points it at Silk Shirt.

"Stop!"

Silk Shirt turns. "What're you gonna do with that, little Bilaganna."

"I want to know what you did to my father."

"You mean that old prospector?" Silk Shirt edges toward his rifle.

"I said stop!"

"You're not really gonna use that thing. You don't even know how." Silk Shirt edges closer.

"I will!" Silk Shirt slowly bends to pick up the rifle.

"You got one shot. Better make it good."

Lesley fires the crossbow, hits Silk Shirt in the shoulder. He drops Yellow Horse, falls back. Lesley runs and grabs Alan's rifle, holds it on Silk Shirt. She moves over to Alan, shakes him. Alan stirs, sits up.

"You okay?"

"Yeah." Alan sees Silk Shirt. He's in pain.

"We need to find the radio. Call the sheriff." Alan gets up starts toward Silk Shirt's rifle.

"That bitch shot me! You gonna let her get away with that?!" Alan reaches for the rifle. Lesley swings the rifle around toward Alan.

"Leave it!"

Alan stands.

"What the hell is going on here?"

"That Bilaganna bitch is crazy!"

"I was going to cover him while you find the radio."

"Hey man, do somethin'! I'm in pain here!"

"Why's he talking to you like that?"

"He must be delirious."

"Fuck, bitch. I ain't delirious! I'm fuckin' pissed!"

"Shut your damn mouth!"

Lesley gets it now. "It wasn't Barry who sent them. It was you."

"Okay, she knows man. Now get me a fuckin' doctor! And not one of those fuckin' Indian medicine men."

"Shut up you ignorant bastard!"

"Dad told you he didn't want to disturb the site. So you sent these two to shut him up."

"He didn't tell me anything."

A voice from behind Lesley interrupts. "I did."

Lesley turns. Shanee stands behind her, pistol in hand. Alan takes the rifle from Lesley.

Shanee steps beside Alan, keeps the gun pointed at Lesley. "You never said anything about killing Arthur. They were supposed to just scare him off."

Alan now points the rifle at Lesley. "You know how pigheaded the old guy was. He'd have never given up."

Silk Shirt writhes on the ground. "Hey! What about me down here? This shit hurts!" Alan motions for Shanee to take care of Silk Shirt.

"This is how you repay dad for all he did for the center? For you."

"Anything I got, I worked for. I learned a lot from him, but I earned my keep."

"You couldn't just wait until dad took off for some other adventure? You had to kill him?"

"I couldn't take the chance. Anyway, he seemed too wrapped up in this one. He hadn't abandoned it like he did the others."

"And all the talk about him helping you establish a name for yourself in archaeology. You two working together."

"That part was all true. Look, this is once in a lifetime. It'll make me famous, like he was."

"Except he didn't have to kill anyone. And I guess now you'll have to kill me too."

Shanee joins them.

"Yeah. What do we do with her?"

"Dr. Whitney is going to have a tragic accident. Just like her father."

Silk Shirt manages to stand. "What the fuck about me?"

"You're going to do what I told you to do."

"I can't get all this stuff outta here by myself! I still need to get to a doctor!"

"Shanee can take Dr. Whitney to the Land Rover. I'll help you get Yellow Horse to the Bronco. Grab what you can and get the rest later."

Shanee leads Lesley off. Alan throws Yellow Horse over his shoulder and follows Shanee and Lesley. Silk Shirt grabs his stuff, stuffs the rest in the bushes, takes off down the canyon trail.

****

A hawk circles above Lost Canyon, gliding on the wind currents, following the movements of Alan, Lesley, and Shanee as they approach the Kiva. They walk across the Kiva floor to the drop off.

"You don't have to do this. I won't say anything to anyone. I'll go back east and forget everything."

"Why would I believe that?

"You know dad and I hadn't talked in years. Now I know what happened. I can go on with my life."

Alan holds Lesley on the cliff edge. "And what guarantees would I have that you wouldn't go straight to the cops there?"

"There are no witnesses. No remains. The sheriff has dropped the search. It's an accidental death. Who's going to believe a Bilaganna girl from back east?"

"There is one witness." Alan looks at Shanee. He points his rifle at her, takes the pistol from her. She's dumbfounded. He empties all but one bullet from the cylinder. Alan hands the gun, barrel first, to Lesley, keeps the rifle trained on her.

"Shoot her."

Shanee screams. "What?! You son of a bitch!"

Lesley backs away. "I can't just kill her."

Alan pulls her back to him, facing Shanee. "It's that or you have your tragic accident."

Shanee pleads. "Don't do it Lesley."

Alan backhands Shanee. "Shut up!"

Alan moves behind Lesley, holds his hand over her hand on the gun, speaks softly, menacingly.

"It was all her idea anyway. She was fucking Arthur to find out what he knew about the Kiva. When he told her he wanted to keep the Kiva a secret, she came straight to me. She's the one who told me about Silk Shirt and Yellow Horse."

Shanee begs. "Lesley don't. He's lying, Lesley."

Lesley's dazed, confused. Alan guides Lesley's hand to point the gun at Shanee. Lesley's hand shakes. Alan's finger moves over her finger on the trigger. Lesley tries to aim the pistol away from Shanee. Alan forces her hand back toward Shanee. Shanee buries her face in her hands, sobbing.

A sudden orgonic surge seizes Lesley. She closes her eyes, releases her grip on the pistol, sees the form of the elementals in her mind. Dust and wind surge. The elementals appear. Lesley grabs onto one of them, hurling about in the wind. The elemental combines its form with Lesley. Alan panics, can't hold onto the gun, drops it onto the ground. Dust and wind swirl around them. Shanee drops to the ground, hidden in the torrent, hunts for the pistol. Lesley drops her arms to her side, her head tilts back, rigid like a Greek statue. Her body begins to rise off the ground, slowly rotating with the tumult. The thick dust hides her. Alan searches through the dust, can see nothing. Shanee desperately combs the ground for the pistol, held fast by the storm, unable to penetrate the wall of wind and then escape. Tenebrous figures appear in the uproar, move about, dancing. Drums. Chanting. Alan fires wildly at the figures, screams at them. Lesley's oblivious to all around her, transported to another time and place with the elemental. Shanee remains crouched close to the ground to avoid Alan's barrage of bullets, walks on hands and knees to try to get behind Alan. Alan spots Lesley, aims the rifle. A shot rings out through the commotion. Alan falls to his knees, sees Shanee, lunges for her. They struggle. Another shot. Everything's still.

The dust settles. Lesley lies on the ground, opens her eyes, stares at the sky, cloud formations framed by beams of sunlight. She notices movement on the ridge above. A figure emerges. Bold Sun? The figure disappears into the sunlight. A hawk swoops down into the canyon, emits a piercing shriek, climbs upward, vanishes. Lesley struggles to sit up, tries to get her bearings. Where is she? She manages to sit up, checks out her surroundings.

About ten feet away, Alan lies face down on the ground, blood oozing onto the back of his shirt. She gets up, goes to Alan, checks his pulse. Something there, but not much. Wasn't Shanee with her? She looks around, doesn't see Shanee. She moves to the cliff edge. At the bottom of the cliff, she sees Shanee's body. What's going on?

****

A flurry of activity. Sheriff Branshee directs deputies and medical personnel, shouts orders. Emergency vehicles fill the canyon, dwarf the Land Rover. A helicopter readies to take off. Lesley sits on the tailgate of an emergency vehicle, covered by a blanket, sipping a cup of coffee. Branshee comes over, grabs a cup of coffee.

"You doin' okay?"

"As well as you might expect."

"We're going to send the helicopter up to look for that black Bronco. We've put out an APB on Silk Shirt and Yellow Horse. Whenever you're ready, one of my deputies will take you back to town."

"What will happen to Alan? To Dr. Hall?"

"If he makes it, he'll stand trial. He'd have died for sure if you hadn't radioed us." A Deputy approaches, pulls the Sheriff aside. Branshee returns.

"The girl was shot before she went off the cliff. Dr. Hall has a lot of explaining to do." The Sheriff moves off. Lesley watches as the helicopter takes off.

****

The hot water in the tub lulls Lesley into a peaceful slumber, her eyelids straining to remain open, but failing. A glass of Malbec awaits on the tub's edge. The events of the past week stream through her mind's eye like a slide show on fast forward.

With Pine Leaf at the hogan.

In the sweat lodge with David, Marianna, and Alan.

With Alan at the Kiva.

In the maze of tunnels with the elementals.

Alan holding her hand on the pistol.

At the Kiva in the dust storm.

Shanee at the bottom of the cliff.

Yellow Horse on top of her.

She screams at the top of her lungs, dives down into the water, curls up into a fetal position. She screams again under the water, releasing all of her breath, tries to stay under the water, tucked into its warmth. She bursts above the surface, gasping for air, releases all the emotion that has been bottled up in her.

She manages, finally, to relax, finishes the glass of Malbec. Sleep beckons. Eyes shut tight. Thoughts spill onto her mind's palette. She sees herself as a young girl with Arthur. Holding his hand walking across campus. Watching him teach a class. Helping her with her homework. He was there for her then. Where was he now, when she needed him most?

B. R. Fleming

13

táá'ts'ádah

****

Lesley's last continental breakfast at the Turquoise Inn exactly resembled the first. Pretty much the nature of the continental breakfast. Lesley tightened the belt on her bathrobe, sipped at the pinion nut coffee, debated whether to eat the remaining piece of Navajo flat bread. On the silent TV, images of the sheriff talking to reporters, photos of Arthur, Alan, Lesley, Shanee, fill the screen. She's become an overnight celebrity, "the heroine of the Kiva caper" the newscaster had called her. Jonathan had seen the news and called immediately, Eastern time, waking her long before her alarm would have sounded. Elliot too had called to check on her, though at a more reasonable hour.

"What have you gotten yourself into out there? You were supposed to be doing some work for the CDC."

"Can I ever do anything simply?"

"No, I guess not. Well, I'm just glad you're okay. You ready to come back to work?"

"Just remember this the next time you think I need a sabbatical."

They both laughed and ended on that note. She'd be catching the next flight out from Durango that afternoon, so she'd better get going. She finished breakfast, dressed, and called the front desk to have someone help with her bags. She really didn't have the energy to carry them herself.

The highway to Durango appeared different to Lesley as she left town. She noticed vegetation, landforms that had never really captured her attention before. What had once seemed desolate now had a raw beauty that could not be appreciated by simply driving through the area. You had to stop and get the dirt and sand and cactus needles in your skin, feel the sun during the dry, hot day, let the moon bleach your skin in the cool breeze of the night. Only then could you really delight in the character of the landscape. She would definitely miss the serenity of the area, but she longed to be back in her apartment, back to her work.

In the distance, in her rearview mirror, an emergency vehicle sped in her direction, lights flashing. She pulled to the side of the road to allow the vehicle to pass safely. As the vehicle neared, she saw it was a sheriff's office Bronco. It slowed and pulled in behind Lesley's Audi. What was going on? A huge Navajo Deputy got out of the vehicle and approached her car. Lesley stuck her head out of the window.

"What is it officer? I wasn't speeding, was I?"

"Ma'am. Are you Dr. Lesley Whitney?"

"Yes."

"Sheriff Branshee would like to see you."

"I'm on my way to Durango. I have a flight to catch."

"He said I shouldn't come back without you. You can follow me, Ma'am."

The Deputy gets back in his vehicle, makes a U-turn on the highway, waits for Lesley on the side of the road. Lesley turns her car around, pulls in behind the Bronco. What could the sheriff want with her now? The officer takes off. Lesley follows.

About thirty minutes later, Lesley and the Deputy pull into the parking lot of the sheriff's office. This had better be important. She would miss her flight and might not get another one out until late that afternoon, if at all. They get out of their vehicles. The deputy holds the door for Lesley as they enter the office. The Sheriff rises to greet them.

"Dr. Whitney. Thank you for coming. I have some information you'll be interested in hearing. Didn't want you to hear it over the phone."

"Did you find my father's remains?"

The Sheriff gestures to a chair. Lesley remains standing. "Well, we found Silk Shirt. He confirmed your story and took us to the remains."

"So it's true. Dad's dead."

"Body decomposes pretty fast out here. Animals, critters do their toll. We only found

part of the skeleton, but we did have the skull. We wanted to get an ID as soon as possible. So we

sent for your father's dental records."

Lesley sits. "Then you've confirmed it."

The Sheriff hesitates. "Yes. And No. Looks like it wasn't your father those two boys killed. We don't know who it was yet, but it definitely wasn't your dad. We combed that area real well--"

"And you still missed this body. How do you know you didn't miss dad's too?"

"We don't. But this one was pretty well hidden. If it'd been accidental, the body would have been more out in the open. Easier to spot."

"I just need to know for sure what happened to my dad."

"That's what I want too. And I'll do everything I can to help you find out."

Lesley stands. "What happens now?"

"I tell you what. You go on and catch your flight. I'll have my guys do another sweep of the area. I'll let you know what we find. If nothing, we'll call it closed."

Lesley heads for the door. Before leaving she turns back. "Oh, Sheriff."

"Yes ma'am."

"I'm really very grateful for all that you and your men have done. I hope you know that."

"I know."

Lesley exits. She knows what she must do next.

****

Lesley knocks on the door to Pine Leaf's hogan, not waiting at her car for an invitation, gets no response, moves around to the back. Mesquite, cacti, other succulents fill the back yard. Lesley tries the back door, opens it, looks in, enters. Lesley admires Pine Leaf's Kachina, other ceremonial and spiritual objects. She peers out a window. In the distance, she sees Pine Leaf walking toward the Hogan. She goes outside, sits, waits. Shuts her eyes.

Pine Leaf arrives, carries a bag, water pouch.

"Yá'át'ééh."

"Yá'át'ééh."

Pine Leaf sits by a large rock, pours cube-shaped objects from the bag. Lesley watches intently. Her gaze begs the question.

"Peyote, daughter."

"A magical pass?"

"Yes. Why do you wait for me, daughter?"

"To enter the second attention and find my father."

"This will be an important journey. I must prepare. You must prepare."

Pine Leaf enters the hogan, returns. "If you are to succeed in this journey you will need the most concentrated effort you have yet produced. When you feel yourself entering the dreaming attention, press the tip of your tongue to the roof of your mouth. Our attention converges on that spot in the daily world. That can be used to intensify your control of the dreaming attention. You must also limit your internal dialogue."

Pine Leaf takes a crystal necklace and wraps it around Lesley's hand, the crystals resting in the palm of her hand. "Keep your hand tight around the crystals. The pressure helps to shut off the internal dialogue. Do you have the Kokopelli necklace?"

Lesley reaches into her shirt and shows the necklace to Pine Leaf. She places it around her neck.

"Good. That will help you resist the temptations of the Scouts." She gives Lesley a gold ring. Lesley slips the ring on her finger. "Remember that the inorganic beings wish to make contact with you, but you must let them know what you wish. They can lead you into many different dimensions of their realm, but only if they know that is where you wish to go. They are the only ones who can lead you to Ahote."

Pine Leaf hands Lesley two dried Peyote buttons. "Chew one of these now." She points to a tree not far from the hogan. "Take off your clothes and sit in the shade of the mesquite tree. Chew the second Peyote button after you sit. If you feel sick, let yourself be sick."

She gives Lesley her water pouch. "Take this water with you. I will come for you when it is time."

Lesley puts a peyote button in her mouth, chews. She reacts only slightly to the taste.

"That is good. The bitterness does not offend you. Go now."

Lesley grabs the water bottle, goes to the mesquite tree, takes off her clothes, sits on a mat in the shade of the tree, against the trunk. She takes a gulp of the water, chews the other peyote button, relaxes. She closes her eyes, drifts. Her hearing becomes intensely acute. Birds chirp vividly. A rattlesnake announces its presence. An ostrich races across a dry creek bed. Meerkats chatter at each other.

Lesley opens her eyes. The once barren-looking desert comes alive. Previously bland colors become opulent, bees become alien ships hovering in the dry heat. Each beam of sunlight streams onto the desert floor, like strands of fiber-optic filament. A scorpion defends itself against a horde of red ants. The ants cheer as the scorpion succumbs to their attack. A roadrunner races across the terrain, is snatched up by a hawk. Lesley misses nothing in the natural drama evolving around her.

Pine Leaf comes, kneels, begins wiping Lesley's body with a damp cloth, whispers to her. "Focus on the most predominant object."

Lesley concentrates on a reflection far across the landscape. Pine Leaf places her hand on the back of Lesley's neck, strikes with her free hand. The reflection brightens, becomes a ball of light. The ball draws Lesley into it. Inside the ball, the light separates into strands, reaching as far as Lesley can see. The light opens up into the pastoral setting of Lesley's earlier dream. Lesley walks alongside the stream, watches as fish and frogs and other creatures swim about and play in the water. A trout swims close to a rock and glides up onto a water-filled indentation. As the trout splashes about in the water, its fins become legs, and the trout stands and walks up onto the rock. Wings now protrude from the trout's body, and the fish begins to flap its wings, cawing at Lesley, as if speaking to her. Lesley stops, realizes this must be a scout summoning her. The fish-bird suddenly shoots into the air, becoming a beam of light like a bottle rocket. Without thinking, Lesley shouts to it.

"Take me with you!"

Lesley flies into the air, directly behind the beam of light, following it into a dark tunnel much like riding a roller coaster. Together, she and the scout maneuver the twists and turns of the tunnel, effortlessly zigging and zagging around the beams of light coming from the opposite direction.

The tunnel abruptly ends and opens into an immense cavern filled with a glowing, gelatinous-looking substance resembling a jelly fish. The beam of light releases Lesley, and she crashes into the jelly, cushioned by the fluid quality of the matter. Lesley bounces off the jelly and floats just in front of it, with the candescent scout hovering over her. The jelly fish fills the cavern in every direction, undulating as if being prodded by ocean waves, fibrous tentacles emanating from the entirety of the globe.

Lesley drifts in the void around the object, fascinated by its enormity, feeling an energetic connection to it. The scout begins to glow brighter, releases a burst of energy that collects Lesley and draws her into one of the tentacles. Again, Lesley follows the scout as it glides along the tentacle leading to the interior of the mass. After a few moments, the tentacle opens into the interior, revealing a convergence of hundreds of tunnel-like appendages shooting out in all directions from the center of the orb. Lesley can't help but wonder where she is and what this is. The voice of the dreaming emissary responds to her thoughts.

"You have reached the interior of an inorganic being, the labyrinth of penumbra. You are floating inside of it. This is the way you move about in this world. The tunnels you see lead to many different experiences and realms of knowledge. Each one will teach something different. The sorcerers of old gained their wisdom and ways through travelling in these tunnels. Some remained and live still in the tunnels. You may choose to live in any of the tunnels you wish or may move from one to another. To stay here, all you must do is state your intent to remain."

Lesley felt the bombardment of energy from all around her, sensed the tunnels pulling at her to enter. She was a ball of energy herself, floating in the orb. Her dreaming state had become ever more real for her, more so than she'd ever felt before. She could imagine the attraction that this state would have for someone like Arthur. The possibility of learning all that the universe had to offer, to delve eternally in the tunnels of the inorganic beings, moving from one to the next when all the knowledge one had to offer was reaped. But how would she be able to find Arthur in this maze of tunnels? The emissary again entered into Lesley's thoughts.

" You will automatically be attracted to any tunnel which contains shared energy with you."

"Shared energy?"

"You share energy with any being with whom you have had contact. Energy is likened to blood. The scout who brought you here you met once before while in the dreaming awareness. That is why the scout could guide you here so easily. To find the one you seek, move to the center of the orb and concentrate on the energy of that being. You will find that one particular tunnel will draw you to it. Let it pull you in. Do not show fear. Do not show hesitation. The inorganic beings want to have a relationship with you. But they will try to trick you if they do not feel that you are serious in your intentions. They will send counter images to distract you from your goal. If you move into the wrong tunnel, you could be lost in it forever. On the other hand, if the inorganic beings connect with you, they may wish to keep you in their world forever."

Lesley thought about the emissary's final statement. If Arthur had shown a real desire to explore the world of the inorganic beings, they may have trapped him there against his will. How would she be able to help him escape, if he actually wanted to escape?

"You alone can only accept or reject the enticements of the inorganic beings. You will not be able to release another being from their grasp if the other being is not willing or able to voice any objection. Remember, always, that anything you say out loud is taken as your intention and becomes real in this world."

Lesley decided she was ready and floated to the center of the orb. She immediately felt numerous tunnels attracting her energy but could not distinguish one with which she connected. A scout appeared and pulled at Lesley to follow it. Lesley responded.

"Take me with you!"

The scout snagged Lesley and guided her from one tunnel to another, seeming to be searching for something. Each tunnel was bathed in a light all its own, radiating from no point in particular with no change in intensity. Their jaunt seemed to last forever, sailing from tunnel to tunnel, until finally, the scout followed a tunnel whose light dimmed until they were surrounded by total darkness. Why had they stopped in this tunnel? Would she find Arthur here?

Lesley searched through the darkness and began to notice shapes forming out of the darkness, globular, beetle-like, grayish-brown figures. The voice of the emissary returned.

"You have entered the shadow world. Though we exist in the shadow world, we provide the light for the tunnels and do the bidding of the tunnels. Each tunnel has shadow beings which perform specific functions for the tunnel. We draw our energy from the tunnels by connecting with them. We cannot exist without each other. You may have seen us as bulges or protrusions on the walls of the tunnels. "

"You mean the tunnels are energy forms?"

"Inorganic beings exist in three forms. The stationary tunnels are the first form. We, the moveable shadows, are the second form."

"And the third form?"

"They exist as the crystalline form. To learn of the third form, you must choose to stay here. To see their form requires a great deal of energy that we would have to provide for you. You would be inextricably linked to us and the tunnels forever."

Lesley began to feel anxious. She wanted to find Arthur, if he really had travelled there, but she wasn't prepared to stay there forever if he had become linked with the crystalline inorganic beings. As Lesley continued thinking, the shadow beings began squirming, their forms modulating, stretching and contracting. Lesley becomes even more anxious, causing the globules to react more violently.

"We feel your energy in whatever form it takes and feed off of it. Try to hold back your emotions. The calmer you remain, the easier you will be able to move around in our world."

Lesley tried to relax. She needed to get back to the center of the sphere to try to find Arthur's tunnel, if he had travelled into one of them. Could the shadow beings get her back to the center? Once she thought this question, she began to feel an overwhelming connection with the shadow beings, an energy draw toward them. Did they not want her to leave?

"To exit the tunnel all you need do is tell the scout your intention to leave. You may leave whenever you wish. But the longer you remain in any tunnel, the more connected you become to it."

As Lesley thought of her intention to leave she found it difficult to say the words. She was becoming more attached to the tunnel and the shadow beings by the second, if time here could be counted in seconds. It could have been days or years that she had been there. Finally she managed to shout the words.

"Let's go!"

The scout had been hanging in the air above Lesley the entire time she had been in the tunnel and immediately returned to its former state, shot down the tunnel, carrying Lesley along behind. They wove their way through the tunnel, faster and faster, the light in the tunnel becoming more brilliant the further they travelled. Lesley could see ahead the opening from the tunnel into the labyrinth, and suddenly they were there, absolutely still, surrounded by the hundreds of appendages, twisting and turning outward from the center of the labyrinth, like the arms of an octopus.

Lesley cleared her mind and thought only of Arthur, tried to recreate her feelings for him as a child. She watched herself following him around the campus, sitting in the classroom during his lectures, fishing with her and Conrad. Some of the tunnels began to react to her, compelling her. Thoughts of him became confused, from her anger over his abandonment of her family to her absolute love of him as his daughter.

More tunnels generated an attraction to her, drawn to her emotional energy. The scout began acting erratically, like a fly buzzing over a dead carcass, flitting from one tunnel to another, waiting for Lesley's next direction. Was it trying to communicate something to her? Bursts of light shot from some of the tunnels, filled the labyrinth with lightning flashes, distracted Lesley from her thoughts. Is that what they were trying to do? Keep her from finding Arthur? Keep her from concentrating? Or were they trying to lure her into a tunnel to keep her there, forever?

The labyrinth became a frenzied tornado of activity. Tunnels thrashed about. Lightning flashes lit the labyrinth like a nightclub mirror ball on speed, dizzying Lesley, distracting her even more. Lesley panicked. How would she find Arthur's tunnel through all of this? Would she be able herself to leave? Her only thought was to ignore the tumult going on around her and concentrate on her love of Arthur.

Gradually, Lesley managed to create a barrier to the distraction, focusing totally on the image of Arthur. From beyond the disturbance she noticed one tunnel remaining still and glowing brightly. Maybe that was what the others were trying to keep her from noticing. The scout immediately noticed her attraction to the tunnel and hovered steadily over Lesley, awaiting her command. That had to be Arthur's tunnel.

"Let's go!"

The scout shot through the tangle of appendages and flashing of lights, tugging Lesley along behind it, weaving in and out of the construct. They entered the tunnel like a bullet train entering a pass through a mountain and instantly adjusted to the pitch and roll of the tunnel's form. As the furor from the labyrinth subsided into the distance, Lesley noticed that this tunnel seemed larger than the others she had entered, and more of the shadow beings appeared to be snuggled into the tunnel walls. They moved furiously through the tube, following the twists and turns, a comet racing through a worm hole in the universe. Then the scout abruptly halted in a particularly enlarged section of the tunnel.

The sudden stop left Lesley somewhat harried. What had caused the scout to stop in this area before reaching the end of the tunnel, if the tunnels even had "ends"? The scout floated just beyond Lesley, appearing to be awaiting a command of some sort, while Lesley acclimated to the new surroundings. Unexpectedly, the scout began rotating, faster and faster, becoming blindingly more brilliant, bursts of light shooting out from it, lighting the walls of the tunnel. Lesley regained her composure, focused her attention on the beams of light which bounced off the walls of the tunnel and then coupled with the closest shadow being, creating an eerie glow glistening throughout the tube.

The tunnel wall radiated with the energy of the newly charged shadow beings who were connecting by strands of light to form heptagonal shapes of varying sizes. The heptagons broke away from the wall and shot out into different directions, filling the tunnel with an unparalleled fireworks display. As the newly formed hexagons darted feverishly throughout the space, a slightly larger blob of energy began to form near the center of the tunnel, emitting a blue hue which made it appear similar to a candle flame

Lesley felt an instantaneous attraction to the blob, compelled to move closer to it. Yet, she could also feel the scout trying to lure her away from the form, using the energy of the heptagons combined with its own to distract her. The see-saw of energy draw left Lesley trapped between the two, and she turned her attention to the scout to try to disconnect from it, losing sight of the blue body. A moment later, a strange, irresistible force grabbed Lesley from behind which she instinctively resisted, only to be spun around and confronted by the energy form.

Fear gripped Lesley. What did the form want with her? Would it trap her in the tunnel forever? Pine Leaf had warned her that the Inorganic Beings would feed off of her fear and to avoid it at all costs. That was all turning out to be easier for Pine Leaf to say than for Lesley to do. Then, a calming sensation overcame her as she gazed into the luminous blue ball of energy. The form pulsated and absorbed all the awareness around it until only the blue form and Lesley remained in the tunnel.

Inside the blue blob, Lesley could see strands of soft, yellowish-white light congealing into an obscure shape, the figure forming like a sculptor molding coils of clay onto a stick frame. Layer after layer of the strands coalesce, a blurred image that Lesley cannot define distinctly but which becomes increasingly human-like. Arms, then legs, then the head become recognizable, and a face appears. Lesley feels a pang of emotion as she stares into the face of her father.

As Arthur communicates telepathically with her, Lesley sees images of her childhood with her
family, of her years growing up through Arthur's eyes.

"Lesley. I know that your life has been an arduous journey for you. And I know that I have not always been there for you."

"Dad --"

"I felt such guilt after Conrad's accident. For letting him down. For letting you down. For letting your mother down. I couldn't face any of you after that. The only thing I knew to do was to pour myself into my work."

"I felt guilty too."

"I know you did. I'm sorry I wasn't there to help you understand that it wasn't your fault in any way."

"Mom helped."

"She always understood you kids much better than I did. Lesley, we don't have much time. The longer you're here the harder it will be for you to leave. This may be the last time you will see me, Les."

"I always loved it when you called me Les." The tears well up in Lesley's eyes.

Arthur smiles. "The inorganic beings here have shown me a path which will allow me to explore the expanses of the universe."

"Immortality?"

"I don't know that. But I know that I will be able to exist here much longer than the little time I would have had remaining in my physical body. I wanted you to know that this is the course that I have chosen to take."

"You brought me here?"

"The inorganic beings have been luring you here for me for this moment. They sent the scouts who brought you here so that I could see you."

"They can manipulate people in the daily world?"

"They have great powers. They've expressed a desire for me to stay with them and share their knowledge with me. They knew I wouldn't go with them until I was able to see you once more."

"Then, this is the last time I'll see you?" Tears now stream down Lesley's cheeks.

"We have no way of knowing that. Just remember, we cannot change the past. We can only experience the future, follow the paths set before us. Know the ways that bring you happiness. Greet them. Exalt in them. Learn the ways of the universe."

Lesley felt a pang of emotion. In one way, she wanted to stay with Arthur to spend the time with him that she had missed for all of those years. But she might never be allowed to return to the daily world once she connected with the crystalline beings.

"Dad, can I go with you?"

"Les, your place for now is in the daily world. You have a lot of life to live before you make that decision."

"But Dad, I'm going to miss you. I've missed so much with you."

"Perhaps one day our energy bodies will again converge. Until then, always remember that I love you, my daughter."

The final image Lesley sees is of her, through Arthur's eyes, at the funeral for Conrad and her mother. So, Arthur had attended the funeral and just didn't want anyone to know he was there. The luminous image of Arthur coalesces into an endless strand of light, zooms off into the expanses of the tunnel.

"Dad!"

The tunnel brightens intensely. Lesley's light is lured to the walls of the tunnel, unable to break free. Heptagons clamor around her, attaching themselves to her, a net of energy holding her in place. She struggles, can't break free. She remembers that she must remain calm, shuts out everything around her, sees the image of the elementals. They appear. She latches onto one, wrestles with it. The heptagons scatter. Lesley writhes and squirms with the elemental, zapping it of its energy. She wills herself to take on her luminous human form. Her light reflects into the ring, radiates through the tunnel, she cries out to the scout, "Let's go!"

The scout whips down the tunnel tugging Lesley away from the elemental and through the winding network of the passage. They wend their way through the tube and reach the labyrinth. The scout carries her toward a ball of light in the middle of the labyrinth. Lesley enters the ball of light, absorbed into it. She imagines herself in the desert on the mat, Pine Leaf next to her, sees herself in front of the mesquite tree. Then, a huge ball of light and . . . Darkness.

****

The flames of the fire danced gently in the cool night breeze. An owl called to its mate from a nest in a Saguro. Coyotes howled in the distance. At the moon? To let the other creatures know they were there? To annoy their enemies?

Lesley lay at the base of the mesquite. Pine Leaf sat next to her, aglow from the light of the fire. Lesley stirred. Pine Leaf lifted her head, adjusted the blanket she had placed on her, cradled her head in her lap. Lesley groggily stared into the flames.

"You have done what few Bilaganna have done, daughter."

Lesley could only think of her meeting with Arthur, or rather Arthur's energy body. How would she ever get back to see him, especially after she returned to New York and didn't have Pine Leaf to help her? Was that really the last time she would ever see her father?

"What have you learned, daughter?"

"My father isn't lost."

"Is that all?"

No. That wasn't all she'd learned. But how could anyone else understand all that she had experienced the past few weeks or grasp the impact it had all had on her. She would never be the same Lesley after this, would never be able to hide behind her research, locked away in her lab, ignoring the outside world. Never be able to hide her true feelings. But she would never have to feel guilty again or try to understand Arthur's disappearance from her life.

"My father isn't lost, but he's not alive either. I'll never see him again."

"Ahote is more than alive. He has become a death defier. He lives in the universe. You can see him again. Continue on the seeing way."

"Will you help me?"

"You can help yourself. You know magic passes. Use them. Nurture them."

Lesley sits up next to Pine Leaf, hugs her. "I'll never forget you."

"I will see you again, one day, daughter."

Lesley gets up. Dresses. Walks away.

B. R. Fleming

14

di′i′′ts'áadah

****

The jet remained motionless on the runway. The predictably unpredictable weather had been playing havoc with all flights out of Denver for the past few days, late summer thunderstorms dropping bucketful's of rain throughout the area.

"Folks, we'll be taking off shortly. The tower says we have a break in the storm, and they're gonna get some of us off the ground. Weather looks good for the rest of our nonstop to JFK. Sit back and relax. Our flight attendants will be serving lunch when we reach cruising altitude. Thanks again for flying with us today."

Lesley fastened her seat belt, sat back, stared out at the mountains surrounding Denver. How would she ever be able to explain what she'd gone through the past few weeks to anyone. She even had a difficult time believing it wasn't all just a dream. Maybe she should just leave it with Arthur disappearing and never being found. Only she, Arthur, and Pine Leaf knew the truth. She hadn't had any trouble not telling Jonathan the truth when they had talked last night.

"Les, I'm really sorry about Arthur. They're sure that he's not just missing?"

"The sheriff has pretty much called off the search. He said he wanted to make one more look in Lost Canyon but that he didn't expect to find anything more."

"Just get back here as quickly as you can. You need to put all of this behind you and move on, get your research going again, get us going again. I've been thinking a lot about that. Us."

"Me too."

"Well, good. I don't like being away from you like this, and I don't want to be any more."

"Let's talk about it when I get back."

She knew what Jonathan meant. Was she really ready to talk about "it." She felt guilty about what had happened with Alan and angry at the way he had turned out. But she had also felt something with Alan that she had never felt with Jonathan. A stirring, an awakening, that sent vibrations through her. She'd never felt that way with Jonathan, even when they made love. Maybe that would be different now. She also knew, though, that she would always be able to depend on Jonathan and knew that he loved her. Well, they would definitely need to have the "us" talk when she returned.

✳✳✳✳✳✳✳✳✳✳✳✳✳✳✳✳✳✳✳✳✳✳✳✳✳✳✳✳✳

Fall had come to Manhattan early. Rain splattered against the bay window in the apartment, whipped by the gusting wind. The hot tea took the chill off the evening, and the glass of Malbec helped, and Lesley relished the change in climate and terrain from the hot, dry, flat Southwest desert plains. If she would ever return she couldn't say. Not for quite a while at any rate. Why would she need to?

Her desk reflected her absence from school and her research and classes. She had managed to separate her personal emails from the hundreds of emails relating to her classes or general school issues or the miscellaneous "junk" that accumulated in a professor's inbox. Emily would sort through those and forward any that Lesley needed to deal with personally.

Elliot had had a thousand questions for her when she had first returned, and she had been choosy about the ones she answered with the truth and the ones she answered with guarded honesty. Some she just ignored completely or changed the subject as quickly as she could, especially the questions relating to Arthur's fate. Who could ever understand or even believe what had happened. She still found herself doubting the reality of all that had transpired. She found herself constantly pulling the Hopi box from the shelf in her study, gazing at the Kokopelli necklace, sometimes for hours on end. She would sometimes wear the necklace under her blouse, sweater, sitting naked in front of the bay window, hoping that having it close would make the entire saga all seem more real.

Being naked seemed all the more natural to her now too. Jonathan had noticed too that she seemed less inhibited than before, and though he didn't know the reason behind her increased libido and lessened inhibitions, he was certainly not going to question or complain. Their love-making had become much more physical and exploratory, and Lesley felt a much more sensual bond with Jonathan. She would sometimes pounce on him the minute he entered the apartment and not let him go until they had both been satisfied, several times.

Just thinking about their escapades made Lesley wish that Jonathan had not had to attend a lecture that evening. She told him to come by, no matter how late it was, when he finished, but now she didn't know if she could stand the wait. The ringing of the doorbell gave her hope that he had foregone the lecture to come by, and she raced to the door and flung it open. The UPS driver standing in the hallway with a medium-sized box wondered why Lesley had met him so happily and why she appeared ready to jump him.

"I have a package for Ms. Lesley Whitney."

"That would be me."

The driver thrusts a clipboard at her. "Sign here please ma'am."

Lesley signs. The Driver leaves. Lesley carries the box to her desk, opens it, pulls out a leather messenger bag. She searches through the bag, pulls out papers, letters. She finds a wallet, opens it, finds a faded photo of her, Conrad, and her mother. Several hundred dollar bills are in the money compartment. She looks further in the bag, finds a pouch containing peyote buttons and a bank register. She opens the register and finds the last entry with a total amount: "$3,453,897." She searches further, finds an envelope addressed to her. She opens the envelope and pulls out a card. The card shows a man walking with a young girl, hand-in-hand, along a sidewalk in a park. The little girl looks up to the man as they walk along, under the words, "Happy Birthday, Daughter." Lesley's eyes begin to tear up. She opens the card, reads the inside to herself.

Dear Lesley, I've never told you enough how proud I am of you. So I wanted to tell you now on your birthday. Thank you for being who you are. I couldn't have asked for a more wonderful daughter. I love you always. Dad.

She settles back in her chair, tears streaming down her cheeks. The phone rings. The answering machine activates.

"You've reached Dr. Lesley Whitney. I'm unable to come to the phone right now. Please leave a message after the tone. I'll get back to you as soon as I can." A tone sounds

"Hello, Ms. Whitney. This is Sheriff Branshee, Montezuma County, Colorado. I hate to leave a message like this, but I thought you'd want to know as soon as possible. We finished that sweep of Lost Canyon and didn't find anything. So we're going to go ahead and list your father's disappearance the way we originally planned as an accidental death. We'll send the death certificate to you. I'll follow up later on to make sure you got this message okay. Bye now."

Lesley stares out through the rain-streaked bay window onto the shimmering Hudson, the lights of New York City reflecting off the seeming still water. A smile breaks through her tears.

B. R. Fleming

Also from B. R. Fleming . . .

A 60'S JOURNEY OF SELF-DISCOVERY.

In **Summertime Blues**, B. R. Fleming creates in Peter Bennings a character searching for himself and for the answers to his life questions. With disappointment and the shattering of his dreams, Peter escapes into music, booze, and sexual adventures. But Peter's universal appeal rests in his quest for answers to the ubiquitous questions about girls and sex and dating and parental restrictions that no one will help answer.

Available from Amazon and other book distributors.

ABOUT B. R. Fleming

B. R. Fleming grew up in the '60's reading sci-fi novels and watching sci-fi movies and was a musician in rock bands that played psychedelic rock and the music of the British invasion. After serving in the US Air Force as a Technical Instructor during the Vietnam War, he returned to civilian life and began a career in teaching, which he has followed since. He lives in Southern California and still plays music and teaches classes in English Lit and Creative Writing in high school, as well as college classes in Teaching the Gifted and Talented and Drama. He studied Screenwriting at the University of California, Irvine, and has completed five feature-length film scripts. His screenplays have been marketed to Sony Pictures and Walt Disney Studios Pictures Marketing.

Mr. Fleming's next project will be *The Colony Trilogy: Torus I; The Colony;* and *The Coming*, a fact-based sci-fi series revolving around colonization of the solar system.

Follow B. R. Fleming:

Twitter: @BFScreenwriter
Facebook: www.facebook.com/bruce.fleming49
Website: http://brflemingauthor.wix.com/brfleming
Email: brflemingauthor@gmail.com

www.ingramcontent.com/pod-product-compliance
Lightning Source LLC
Chambersburg PA
CBHW050325110726
47899CB00007B/2380